Those Who Scream

A Novel by 30 Writers

I0694571

Those Who Scream: A Novel by 30 Writers

Copyright © 2022 Thirty West Publishing House & respective authors

All rights reserved.

This is a work of fiction. Names, characters, businesses, places, events, locales, and incidents are either the products of the author's imagination or used in a fictitious manner. Any resemblance to actual persons, living or dead, or actual events is purely coincidental.

ISBN-13: 979-8-9861105-0-9

Cover art: "Seeing Ghosts on Roads of Loss and Losses to Come," by Mickey Haist Jr., Winner of the #antiwrimo Cover Art Contest.

Printed in the U.S.A.

For more titles and inquiries, please visit:

www.thirtywestph.com

Witness the journey online #antiwrimo

Preface

Hello.

You may have found this book through the means of a silly hashtag, #antiwrimo. What exactly is that? Unfortunately, I'll have to explain another acronym in which it emerged. 'Oh, come on,' you may be asking. 'What does a fancy acronym have to do with a piece of fiction?' I'll tell you one thing, it's a critical aspect of how this book came to be. Allow me to explain.

For those who don't know, National Novel Writing Month (NaNoWriMo) was founded by Chris Baty in the San Francisco Bay in 1999. It began as it still is today: writing 50,000 words in the single month of November. What was more of an accountability experiment, has since been incorporated as a non-profit organization. They are sponsored by national and international donors and are underpinned by hundreds of thousands of authors. I, personally, have never taken part in this event, but I know many that have, and the community is strong and diverse. You may have done so 'unofficially' by just, well, authoring a novel. But in the confines of a single month, it is a massive challenge and an extreme source of stress. So, I wanted to approach November 2021 on a polar opposite path. Why not just have many writers do a little bit of manageable writing instead?

And thus, AntiWriMo was born. Nice, good going. Now, where are all the writers? In a similar avenue as Mr. Baty, I asked my community of Thirty West writers initially. It was received with supportive fervor yet was tough to garnish members of the roster at first. Given its proximity to the holidays and COVID-19 afflictions, I spread this idea so thin, that it was almost doomed to fail. But a couple of dozen writers and then some answered the call, out of nearly 100 inquiries. 'Maybe this thing wasn't going to be so bad after all,' I imagined.

A team was solidified in October 2021. I joined the ranks as well and the concept overtook me like a spell. Whenever I was clocked out of work, I'd immediately pivot to the spreadsheets, documents, and other small errands that were required. I cared not about Halloween weekend, just making sure that midnight on November 1st was set and ready to go. No one expected what was to come from this, and quite frankly, neither did I. Blind idealism, anyone? I gave no prompt, no outline, not even a single character. A novel with an ever-changing premise and genre, chockfull of distinctive styles. What more could one ask for? If this was to be the inaugural AntiWriMo, why not just go bonkers?

All that was asked was to write 1,000-2,000 words. Sounds easy enough, right? Not exactly. We're all just people with our normal schedules and obligations. After a week or so, it started to feel like being on a boat without a sail. I was impressed how everyone piggybacked, but frustrations were becoming clear. Yet every day, the Google Doc grew a bit longer. These 'chapters' gave me faith that this experiment was able to succeed.

And guess what? We made it. December 1st came around and a collective sigh of relief came out. Some say 'The End' is truly not the end. The road of edits continued after a short break for holiday festivities. Believe me, we all needed it. Engaged in casual and professional debriefings and even a roundtable discussion on Zoom. Sometimes it's good to have an open forum where ideas can generate organically and in real-time.

While a corporate publisher would vie to assimilate a style guide or template, we locked in each writer's voice and style. You will see how the prose ebbs and flows. Sometimes even fractures apart or diverges into tangents unforeseen. I tried to market this from the beginning: What does it feel like to fall back in love with the process of writing? Additionally, we hosted a cover contest. That alone endured a long road of voting and considerations, but we enjoyed how folks interpreted this novel, visually. I think it captures the aesthetic quite well.

Those Who Scream is a novel about dishonest opportunities, ancestral secrets, conjuring horrific deities, and the distinctive protagonist, Molly Hammersmith. It will resound off every turn of the page. There is much to indulge in. I implore you to look at the header of each section and see the names of the authors. The novel concludes with biographies, so please take some time to follow their writing journeys. I can cosign many of their works and publications. Friends, clients, and just neat people that have lent their time and abilities. Let us know what you think, too. We'd love to see your ratings and reviews on Goodreads, Amazon, etc. Even emails to the press will be appreciated.

I'm unsure if this is the only time this will happen. I do not know if I'll have the honor of working with 30 writers on such a lengthy project again. This was a confluence that was unique only to 2021, a year that had many uncertainties and setbacks. The experiment succeeded and we thank you for taking a chance with this book. Just as we once did many moons ago. Small press has no expiration date.

Sincerely,

Josh Dale & the
#antiwrimo crew

Those Who Scream

1.

If you play stupid games, you'll always win stupid prizes.

As she made her way toward the end of the dirt road, Molly replayed her grandmother's warning in her mind. This half-assed journey was one of the worst ideas that Molly had conjured up in some time, and that's saying a lot. Exploring foreign cities at night, amongst the pickpockets and other hidden threats. Or, when Molly decided it would be a great idea to take a semester off from college and live with her boyfriend for one month (who turned out—surprise—to have a history of jumping into relationships with women who were desperate for a boyfriend). Molly tended to have a history of poor and reckless decision-making. Such was the case for her current hasty plan of "reinventing" her life once again. But instead of running off to a sunny island far away from the confines of Kentucky or becoming a Buddhist to find peace within herself, Molly took an odd job deep within the south of Georgia. She had found this job on a job board outside of her local library. She had spent the day wandering the stacks of books, searching for inspiration as to what would be her life's next big turn of events. She had never heard of a Cemetery Caretaker before, and honestly, she didn't fully know what that line of work would entail. Regardless of her naivety, Molly picked up the receiver and dialed the number listed on the wanted ad. An old Southern man's voice answered, roughly, as if he had just smoked ten packs of cigarettes at once. After a loud hacking of his lungs, Mr. Nash explained the main details of the job and how "not a damn one of these people knows about caring for those who can't care for themselves." Though he was hesitant to hire a woman to do manual labor, Molly insisted, and pleaded, to Mr. Nash that she would be perfect as a caretaker. She had a little experience with hard labor, like when she helped her grandmother care for a small chicken coop. She also tended to the modest vegetable garden that she helped plant on the side of the house, right outside Molly's bedroom window. "I can do this," she told Mr. Nash confidentially, "I'm willing to do whatever I need to make this work. I'm not afraid to get my hands dirty." After a long pause, and what sounded like a long drag of a cigarette, Mr. Nash let his decision be known with a simple yet effective "alright then." But before Molly had a second to begin packing, Mr. Nash ended the phone call with a warning, "don't bother bringing anything other than books or paper, we ain't got no distractions out here and we're keeping it that way."

When Molly thought of Georgia, she imagined sitting on a front wrap-around porch at night, listening to the music of crickets, while eating delicious peaches. She would be fanning herself from the summer heat while watching the Spanish moss-covered trees light up in bursts of amber sporadically from the million lighting bugs that called it home. Naturally, all of her southern fantasies of a charming lifestyle came crumbling down with the first few bites of mosquitoes and the overpowering heat of the afternoon sun. As Molly drove towards her new life as a cemetery caretaker, massive oak trees surrounded each side of the road, as if Mother Nature had built Her own massive wooden fence to keep intruders out. There didn't seem to be many homes nearby, as she mostly spotted general stores and gas stations forgotten by time. The nearby town of Moultrie was about ten miles away but was mainly a farming community. The reality was that Molly had officially left society and moved deep into the unwanted nether region of South Georgia. There, regardless of whatever she imagined, Molly was going to live a very lonely and quiet lifestyle. This fact didn't frighten or deter her from finally reaching her final destination. She parked and stepped out from the driver's side of her beat-up black Ford Explorer. As she walked onto the pebbled path that marked the entrance to the Scarlet Maple Cemetery, she inhaled a deep breath before releasing it out along with any trepidation she was carrying. There, amongst the trees, dirt, and grime, were hundreds of tombstones. All shapes and sizes, some covered in sticky moss and some as grimy as if coated with a fresh coat of black paint. If Molly hadn't been offered the job, she would have guessed that this cemetery was abandoned, based on the neglected state it was in. There were also small mausoleums, with family names carved into each arch, such as ANDREU and BURKE. Broken stained glass windows lined the floors inside. Wild animals and insects had also made their nests atop burial chambers. The entire cemetery was a complete disaster. How could anyone allow their family member's grave to fall into such a disheveled state?

As she continued walking, careful not to step onto any thick brushes of pine needles in case of snakes, she spotted the caretaker's home. She hurried towards the front porch, then climbed up the short wooden steps as her boots loudly announced her arrival. When she reached the front door, she knocked lightly.

"Mr. Nash?" she said, "sir, it's Molly. I'm here. I parked down the road, I hope that's..."

The front door opened ajar.

"Hello?" she said

Molly put her right hand on the door, pushing it all the way open, revealing an empty living room. This room looked like it was stuck in the 1970s, with its plush round carpet that was plopped right in front of a high-back velvet reading chair. Peaking just over the top, was a semi-bald head, with little grey hairs randomly springing forth like pesky weeds. A thin string of smoke was floating up towards the ceiling. Tiny fragments of ashes fell to the floor beneath the man's feet.

"Mr. Nash?" Molly said while creeping closer. *Perhaps Mr. Nash is hard of hearing, being an older man and all,* Molly thought. When Molly reached the side of the chair, she expected him to jump up or curse in response to being startled. Instead, Molly came face to face with a stiff lifeless body. Mr. Nash was dead, yet his fingers held onto the barely lit cigarette that was near to its filter.

2.

Molly had seen dead things before. When Molly was young, she and her grandmother kept two chicken coops behind the house. One morning a raccoon got into the older coop and killed half their hens. All but one of the birds had been torn apart and smeared across the grass behind the house. Molly and her grandmother picked up the pieces and threw them in a 5-gallon bucket. The chickens from a newer coop clucked and scratched as if nothing had happened. Even as a girl, Molly was struck by the way the living could face death and just get on with life. The old-coop hen who survived was pretty gnawed up. The poor thing was missing a foot, and one of its wings hung almost to the ground by an overstretched ligament. Her grandmother always made the best of things though. She slaughtered it, plucked it, and tossed it into a soup. Molly never forgot the taste of that soup—it tasted perfectly normal, delicious even.

Mr. Nash wasn't the first dead person she'd seen either. Molly was young when her father died, so her only real memory of him, the only one she was sure hadn't been implanted by one of her grandmother's stories, was seeing his oversized body shrouded and stuffed into an undersized coffin. It wasn't a happy memory, but it wasn't sad either. It just was. In her memory, she could feel her grandmother's arms around her. She could see her grandmother's eyes glazed with tears. She missed Kentucky. What the hell had she come to Georgia for anyway?

Too late now. She was here, staring at a dead man, trying to figure out what to do next. The only thing moving in the room was smoke from Mr. Nash's cigarette. Molly was half-tempted to take the last drag. Her other half was sickened by the swollen, dead fingers holding the cigarette. She could see blood beginning to pool on the man's chin. She imagined it pooling in his feet, in his chair. She slid a monstrous porcelain ashtray from a side table under the burning cigarette. The ash fell and covered one eye of a gawking cartoon squirrel glazed into the bottom of the ashtray.

Molly took a renewed look around the room. A few faded prints of generic landscape paintings hung from the wood-paneled walls. The room was lit by a couple of corroded brass wall sconces. Next to the squirrel ashtray, Molly saw a set of epoxy salt and pepper shakers, each in the shape of a squirrel. She picked up the pepper shaker and shook it. It was empty. A huge black phone sat on a short desk in the corner of the room. The handset was covered in grime and shorn skin cells. The numbers were all but worn off.

Molly thought she should call the cops. Then she remembered the scummy sheriff who had pulled her over on her way into town. She was only a few miles from the cemetery when she'd seen the flashing lights in her rearview. She pulled onto the gravel and fished her driver's license from a little change purse she kept on the passenger seat. She flexed her face into a tried-and-true smile—the one she'd used to sidestep a thousand fixes, jams, and binds—and rolled down her window.

The cop had his well-rehearsed routine. He kicked her tires for a god-knows-what reason, then he sauntered over, spread-legged like some goddamn cowboy, and sneered at her.

"Come a long way, young lady?" he'd said. He spoke with a sort of exaggerated, bullshit southern accent that must have been written and produced in the deep, deep south of southern California. This was a man who missed the point of every joke he'd ever heard. This was a man who wore his authority like a hairshirt, twitching and itching at anything that rubbed him the wrong way. And he wasn't even that much older than her.

"Plates say Kentucky, don't they?" Molly said. She'd already decided her put-on smile wasn't going to work. She held her ID out to him.

"Mmm. So that's how they do it in ol' Kentucky?" the cop said under his breath. He looked over her license. "So far as I can see, you ain't a liar. You got registration for this vehicle? What business you have down here?" He looked up at her and spit something deep brown into the grass beside him.

"Does everyone who visits this town have the pleasure of meeting you, Officer?" Molly tossed her ID into the passenger seat. While she rummaged through her glove box, looking for her registration, she leaned forward for a look at the officer's name badge. "Officer Benchley?" she said. She had let herself spit out his name. She'd turned his name into a challenge. She hung her registration out the window at him.

"Deputy Sheriff Benchley, young lady." The sheriff snatched the registration from her hand. He barely glanced at it and tossed it back into the car.

"I just took a job down here," Molly said, finally capitulating.

After she said it, the sheriff stepped back and then nearly fell over in a kind of phony, practiced laugh. "So, you're a liar after all," he said.

The idiot wouldn't stop his false laughter. He even used his actual hand to slap his actual knee. When he finally got a grip, he continued. "I hate to be the bearer of bad news, ma'am, but the Corning plant's been closed for about 15 years." Molly stared at him, waiting for him to finish. He kept hollering. "You best get back on the highway, ma'am. Tallahassee is about 70 miles that-a-way," he said, chopping the air with his arm.

"Took a job at a cemetery a few miles off. Working for Mr. Nash. You heard of him?" Molly said. She spoke quietly, but she'd said enough to stop Sheriff Benchley's fit of laughter. She'd stopped him hard and fast. His smile shut up into a scowl. His forehead curled up against itself. She could almost see the blood pumping out of his face and hands, retreating into his body to shield his organs from an unnamed threat. It was fear, and she knew because it was contagious.

"I think you better keep on and get out of town, young lady," Sheriff Benchley said. He backed toward his cruiser. "I think you better get the hell out of Dodge. And don't talk about no Mr. Nash where anyone can hear you."

And with that, the sheriff had slammed his car door and peeled off down the road to abuse the next unsuspecting out-of-towner. At the time, Molly thought the sheriff had suddenly been cowed by her mention of the great and powerful Mr. Nash. She thought maybe Nash was some kind of bigwig around here. Maybe the Nash family owned one of those sin-stained old houses, dripping with Spanish moss, set on acres of blood-drenched hills. But now, staring at Mr. Nash's dead body, she knew the sheriff must've been reacting to something else about Mr. Nash.

She held the handset of the old phone up to her ear. She wouldn't dial the police. Instead, she pulled a small piece of paper from her pocket. Not long ago, she'd scrawled a phone number across that paper. She'd written it quickly, hopefully, and just about flew into her car to drive down to Georgia and start over. It was Mr. Nash's number, and now she was on Mr. Nash's phone. She knew she'd get a busy signal, but she dialed anyway. A couple of odd clicks and the busy signal never came.

"Hello?" Molly whispered. It was so quiet—just her and the dead man. Something on the other end of the line crackled. She heard what sounded like low breathing.

3.

"Hello?" she tried again, this time in a normal voice. There was more clicking; there was more silence.

"Hello!" Molly finally yelled, losing her temper, vestiges of a childhood where alcohol flowed like water and tempers were easily lost.

"Well, *bless your heart,* you don't need to holler," responded a voice. "*You* called *me*, remember?"

The Southern drawl sounded indignant, and Molly felt a rush of relief. Here, finally, was some company in the lonely room with its dead occupant and its dying cigarette, where the quiet was so thick it was liquid. She grasped onto the sound like a drowning man on a life raft.

"I'm so sorry, I must have dialed the wrong number," she blurted. "I thought I was dialing..."

"Well, this is the operator, honey. Can I patch you through somewhere?"

Molly took a moment to gather her bearings. There were some lines crossed in this backward town; clearly, something had changed since her last conversation with Mr. Nash.

Besides his untimely death, of course.

But now she was here, now there was no turning back, and Molly felt unmoored, an alien on new terrain. Tendrils of loneliness crept in as she considered the question at hand. She suspected the correct answer was, obviously, something to the effect of "the police station." Molly didn't know much about forensics, but she *did* watch television, and this, after all, was all those detectives tended to call a "crime scene."

"Honey? You ok?"

Now that she wasn't being yelled at, however, the woman on the other end of the phone sounded far kinder. Her voice brought to Molly's mind an image of red gingham, pies cooling on windowsills, infants with wide bonnets in old wooden cradles. Her voice was *maternal,* and as Molly enjoyed the visions of a Southern upbringing that had never been her own, she found she was in no rush to request Sheriff Benchley and his snide laugh.

"I'm ok," she responded. "I just had a fright."

The operator laughed.

"Goose walked over your grave?" she asked conversationally. Molly shuddered and squeezed her eyes shut, warding off the sight of Mr. Nash and the cigarette's last stand.

"I'm new in town," she managed. Now that Molly had grown used to the woman's presence over the phone, she was reluctant to be left alone in the quiet again. The quiet scared her in a way the corpse did not.

"Well, welcome to Scarlet Maple!" the operator said, delighted. "I've been here forever. We take care of each other here. Lord knows there's not much else to do!"

Molly was struck, suddenly, with a wave of homesickness so strong, that it knocked the wind from her chest. It was something her grandmother would say. Hell, her grandmother probably *had* said it once or twice during the lengthy court battle to gain custody of her granddaughter. Lord knows there wasn't much else to do.

"The cemetery..." Molly began, and paused, unsure how to continue.

"Oh, are you looking for your kin?" the woman asked sympathetically. "I'd love to help, darlin', but our boneyard has been abandoned for some time now. There isn't anyone for me to connect you to."

Confused, Molly shook her head, as if the operator could see her.

"But I spoke to Mr. Nash? The caretaker?"

There was a long silence; it stretched on uncomfortably.

"Where did you say you came from, dear?"

The drawl, this time, had lost all warmth. It sounded hostile. It sounded *unwelcoming.*

"Uh...Kentucky?" Molly volunteered, baffled as to the woman's change of tone.

Another pause; a loud exhale.

"If I was you, I'd forget that number you dialed," the operator said thinly. "I'd forget all about Scarlet Maple and the cemetery and Mr. Nash. I would just *go*."

At that, the line cut off, and Molly was alone again.

"What the hell was that?" she asked rhetorically. Already expecting the outcome, she redialed the same number and waited. No busy signal; no clicking; no breathing; no operator.

"Well, *now* what?" she questioned again, vaguely wondering if this entire thing was a weird Southern hazing ritual. How else to explain everyone's odd reactions?

Reluctantly, she shifted her gaze to the corpse beside her, its cigarette having finally given up the ghost. Nothing had changed during the duration of her phone call; Mr. Nash was still dead.

A thump. Something heavy dropped onto her shoulders.

Molly's scream echoed through the stuffy room, shattering the quiet with painful intensity. She whirled in circles, batting at her head and neck, trying to evict the talons of whichever beast from the bowels of Hell was clinging to her back.

The kitten evaded Molly's flailing hands and finally leapt gracefully to the floor with a trill of annoyance.

"Kitty!" Molly scolded. "You *scared* me!"

Heart pounding, she bent to scoop up the kitten, travel-sized and black as pitch. It purred mightily; it nudged her fingers for food.

"Well, *someone's* been feeding you," Molly remarked. "Is your mama around?"

The kitten burrowed deeper into her chest, and Molly felt better in a way she had not since her last breakup.

"Mine never was, either" she confided. "Always found her at the bottom of a bottle, though."

The purring subsided as the kitten lapsed into sleep, and Molly grew aware of the uncomfortable silence once again.

"Well," she said slowly, thinking aloud, looking at the slumbering cat, starting to pace the floor. "Here are our options. We can wait here for someone to find us. We can call the police. Or we can go somewhere else ourselves to bring back help."

The kitten had no opinion to offer.

Continuing to pace in circles, Molly considered her surroundings; she considered her entire trip to Scarlet Maple thus far. She considered that the longer she waited, the longer she'd be in a house with a decaying corpse, and *that* was the only consideration it took to make her decision.

"C'mon, Annabel," she told the sleeping kitten nestled in the crook of her arm. "We're getting out of here for now. Let's bring the cavalry and figure out what the *hell* is going on."

Molly backed out the entryway the same way she had come in, heavier by one cat and lacking one job offer, her eyes never leaving Mr. Nash's body. On the porch, heebie-jeebies finally getting the best of her, Molly whirled around and prepared to dash down the path to her Explorer.

She could see the entrance to the cemetery clearly; she could read the sign, even backward, from where she stood. She saw the same pine trees she had passed on the way in, the same beat-up road she had traveled to get here. What Molly could *not* see was her black SUV, and it took her a comically long time to understand that neither she nor the kitten would be going *anywhere* quite yet.

Her car was gone.

4.

Molly smiled uncomfortably. She squeezed the kitten a little bit and it went *mweh*.

"Oh, fuck me," she said.

She surveyed it all. The pine trees, the graveyard, the shitty porch. She felt herself still smiling, a sort of totally-doomed smile, imagining herself from an aerial shot way up high, a crisp nothingness in all directions for miles and miles. Ten miles from Moultrie. Then another five to something less shitty. She could walk ten or fifteen miles, maybe, she thought. A mile is like fifteen minutes walking, so a hundred and fifty minutes. Less than three hours. That sounded doable—it was nothing compared to her old cross-country days (state champ!) but definitely a lot now after a few months of aimlessness and late-night television. In any case, the sun was at a low angle. Dusk seemed to be coming early. Or maybe she had simply lost track of time. She'd have to wait until morning.

She went back inside the house and plopped Annabel right next to the old telephone. Molly had always liked the image of a cat sitting next to a telephone. She picked up the receiver and, as she expected, there was no dial tone. Everything that would happen felt inevitable, at that moment. And it was only a matter of time before she found out what that all would be. She just hoped it wasn't a creepy guy in a mask, like in the movies her mama used to watch on TBS, drinking gin and smoking. She could almost smell the juniper berries and harsh ethanol, almost taste it. The haze, the murmur from the old boxy television, her mama calling out for something, moaning...She slammed the receiver down and it *dinged* lightly. She noticed her breathing: fast and shallow. The precursor to panic. She had to get a grip.

"Get a grip!" she yelled. It felt stupid and good. She was alone and fucked so it felt like a good time to scream and be loud. Annabel looked at her, then nuzzled the phone. "I'm getting a grip!" Molly yelled. Her voice sounded warm and wet. She read, once, in an issue of her little brother's *Teen Vogue*, about how positive affirmations can change your brain. Your thoughts can affect your feelings. You can convince yourself of anything. If you don't take care of yourself, who will? "I'm not gonna die here!" she shouted, firmly, stamping her foot. She spun around and pointed wildly, half-expecting to catch some creeper with razor wire and disarm him with her prescience. But no, nothing. Her shout echoed and died, then it was quiet. Annabel snored softly.

Molly got out her pad of paper (thankful to old Mr. Nash for suggesting she bring that, at least) and made a to-do list. She started with a few things she had already completed and immediately scratched them off, to feel a sense of progress and optimism – another trick from *Teen Vogue*:

~~Break up with that asshole Darren~~
~~Get tires rotated~~
~~Go to job in Georgia~~
~~Get a pet cat~~
Food + water
Blankets? Bed?
Pack for morning
Get rid of the creepy old man corpse
*Find shovel(s)^*

The house was old and musty, but well-stocked. She imagined finding only bare cupboards and mouse droppings, having to uncover a rifle and hunt for varmints to eat, but, thankfully, the fridge and shelves boasted a variety of weird, canned goods and potted meats. It wouldn't be pleasant eating, but it would be something. She twisted a knob on the stove and the electric coil burner hummed to life. The faucet let flow cold, clear water. The toilet was flushed and refilled without a problem. She would be fine. "I'll be fine!" she shouted, half-expecting to hear a sneering chuckle somewhere in the other room. But, again, no. She was alone.

There was a guest room. There were lamps, extra blankets, a whole shed full of, what else but, gravedigging tools. A tea kettle and some old bags of Lipton. A tin of Danish butter cookies. A steak knife was tucked in her waist band, just in case. She felt curious about this Old Mr. Nash. How did he get the job listing all the way up in Kentucky? Why did that Officer Sheriff Deputy Benchley-whatever act so weird about him? And the phone operator? Molly imagined an infinitely stupid conspiracy: a nearly-teenaged cop and an elderly phone operator plotting the death of the mysteriously wealthy cemetery caretaker, all going to plan until Molly Hammersmith shows up to blow the whole plot to hell with her shape-shifting kitten...She pulled herself out of the daydream, standing slouched by the kitchen sink, impressed at how the absence of cell phones and computer screens seemed to allow for a much more vivid imagination. When was the last time she daydreamed like that? Dust floated around. She went back to her list.

As the sun glared orange in the west-facing windows, things started to feel downright cozy. The house seemed well-built, judging by its lack of creaking floors, its fully intact windows, its quaint, homey decorations: doilies and needlepoints, and even a big wooden duck decoy on the mantle. If it weren't for, well, all the creepy and threatening bullshit, she'd have been excited about staying there. It was perfect – nearly perfect. Unfortunately. Molly packed her old Jansport with some crackers and sardines and an old thermos of water and placed it enticingly by the front door. She just had to get through one night, she told herself. And things weren't so bad.

The crickets started chirping in full force as she sat on the couch in the living room, facing Mr. Nash's slumped body and sipped her tea. Annabel leapt up and made himself a bed in Mr. Nash's lap. Molly frowned.

"No, no, okay? No way," she said. She half-crouch scooted across the room to shoo the little kitten off, then settled back in on the couch. Annabel sniffed the shovel propped up near the back door, then scampered over and jumped onto Molly's lap.

"Well, Annabel," Molly said, "I guess I'm gonna have to dig a grave..." She kissed the little fluffernutter on the head. "...Again."

5.

"Remember, Molly: Men are like carousel horses. They might come in different lacquers, one saddle might be bigger than another, but they all take you up, down, and nowhere."
—Darleen Hammersmith, three gins in, to Molly, age nine.

Memories of her childhood crept into Molly's head at the most inopportune times. Had her mother been wrong, though? Darleen's gin-pickled thoughts did not always lack wisdom. Was Molly taking yet another ride to nowhere?

Molly and Hugh approached the firehouse: a handsome, three-bay, red brick building with a clock tower. A crimson and gold ladder truck gleamed in one of the bays. A similarly colored ambulance shone in another. The third bay stood empty. Hugh pulled into the small visitors' parking area, his delivery truck taking up nearly the whole lot. Summer sun gleamed off Molly's thighs in the mini-dress she'd been wearing the day she and Ryan first met, the memory of which she subconsciously hoped to rekindle.

Had Molly been inclined to shame, she might have felt ashamed asking her neighbor Hugh for a ride to see Ryan. Hugh, who always looked at Molly like she was a lost goddess he hoped to ferry back to heaven. Hugh also happened to have a brother who worked at the same firehouse as Ryan. Molly *needed* to see Ryan. Needed to explain about Darren. Needed to beg forgiveness. The fact was, Molly hadn't even had to ask Hugh for a ride. She'd told him she needed to see Ryan, knowing that she and Ryan were involved, and he'd offered, saying he was headed that way to have lunch with his brother anyway.

"What's your plan, Molly?" Hugh asked.

Why anyone ever assumed she had a plan bewildered her.

Plans were for people who feared the future. Molly feared needles, rattlesnakes, and anyone who reminded her of her mother—but she did not fear the future. In her experience, whatever was next was almost always better than what came before it.

"We ring the doorbell," Molly said.

"Have you ever been to a fire station before?" Hugh asked.

Molly thought. There'd been a "Touch-A-Truck" event for children at her elementary school once. The firefighters had let the children sit in the driver's seat and turn on the lights. She had been so enamored of the truck, Mrs. Sugarloaf had to pry Molly's little fingers off the steering wheel and carry her away—flailing and screaming "My truck! My truck!" Molly smiled at the memory. Then, because memories traveled in strange groups, she remembered what it was like being naked with Ryan. The corrugated glory of his body. Blond, buff Ryan in candlelight and a smile was the only heaven she knew.

"No."

"Was good to see you smile just now," Hugh said. "Thinking of your fireman?"

"No," Molly lied.

"We'll need a reason if you plan to come in. Fitch will let me in no problem, but you—" He stammered. "You said your fireman doesn't want to see you."

Molly remembered Ryan's face when he'd learned that the child she'd miscarried two months earlier was Darren's and not his. How he'd wept and asked her to leave. Told her never to contact him again. Why the hell had Molly gone and told him? What was the point of true love if you couldn't tell the truth? What would have been the point of explaining that she miscarried because Darren was a mutant—a fact he'd disguised long enough to wreck her life like he'd wrecked his motorcycle? Wasn't it funny how the carousel always stopped at the same place it started? Wasn't it funny how not-love could kill true love? Wasn't it funny how people believed you had to die to go to hell?

"If he sees you through the window," Hugh was still talking,

"And believe me, he will. What then?"

Molly didn't think so much as look around, as though the cab of a package delivery truck would hold the answer to Hugh's question. Her eyes fell on a box-cutter in the center console. What solution didn't bring fresh problems? She grabbed the box-cutter, exposed the blade, and dragged it two inches across her left thigh. Anyone else would have screamed, but she didn't. An urgent-looking quantity of blood rolled down her leg.

Hugh went white at the sight of Molly's leg.

"You want me to carry you?"

Molly did not want Ryan to see her in another man's arms. "No!"

"Okay. Here goes."

Hugh held her left elbow as Molly limped to the visitors' entrance and pushed the buzzer.

The door opened instantly.

Ryan met them in the vestibule.

"What happened to your leg?" Ryan asked, picking Molly up and holding her like a baby, carrying her through the station, and setting her down, without jostling her even a little bit, onto the cot in the back of the ambulance.

"Box cutter," Molly said, wrinkling her nose at the sharp, rubbing alcohol smell of the ambulance.

"Anything—the blade or anything—still in the wound?"

"No."

"What were you doing when you got this cut?"

"I was holding a box cutter."

"You were cutting a box?"

"What difference does it make?"

"Did you cut yourself by accident?"

Molly hesitated. "Yes."

"You're sure?"

"Yes, I'm sure."

Molly could see in his face Ryan didn't believe her.

"Are you allergic to anything besides bee stings?"

"No." She felt strangely happy he remembered she was allergic to bee stings. She'd only mentioned it once, early in their relationship, on a bike ride in the park.

"Are you or could you be pregnant?"

He knew she'd had an IUD placed immediately after the miscarriage. He'd been holding her hand when the doctor put it in, and he'd paid for it before anyone asked for money.

"Are you serious?"

"I have to ask."

Molly kept thinking about last night when Ryan carried her from the couch in his living room to his bed. His movements had been the same as when he carried her into the ambulance. She remembered the thrill of it, marveling that Ryan carried her as though she weighed no more than a kitten. Now here he was asking her all these antiseptic questions.

"No, I'm not pregnant."

When he saw that Hugh had followed them, Ryan said to Hugh: "Do you mind?"

Hugh didn't move.

"Please," said Molly.

Hugh walked back to the station house.

Ryan pulled on a pair of blue rubber gloves, tore open a packet containing a large, sterile gauze pad, elevated her injured leg, and applied firm-but-gentle pressure on the cut.

"Have you been drinking?"

"My mom didn't exactly make drinking look glamorous."

"Have you had any alcohol today?"

"No!"

"Have you taken any illegal substances today?"

Molly had not. She hadn't so much as smoked a joint in five years. "You know me!"

"Have you engaged in the use of any illegal substances today?"

She had asked for this. She had told him about Darren. It was her fault they'd become strangers.

"No."

"You should have a tetanus shot."

The lack of affection in his voice hurt more than the gash and scared her more than a tetanus shot.

"Are you going to give me a shot?"

"You'd have to go to the hospital for that. Or your doctor." He continued applying pressure to the wound.

"I don't have a doctor." Molly had been too healthy and too broke to see a doctor regularly.

"It's still bleeding. You'll probably need a stitch or two," he said, lifting a corner of the gauze.

Molly studied his face for feelings. The way he was looking at her, she might as well have been a CPR training dummy.

"I'm sorry about everything," Molly said.

"You'll have to sign some papers saying you don't want to be taken to the hospital and stuff."

"Ryan?"

Molly looked for an instant at the blood all over her leg and on the gauze.

"What?"

Her body felt cold. Then she saw spots.

She dreamed while she was out. A thick, wonderful dream. She dreamed of Ryan smiling and holding her at the top of a mountain. Caressing her face. It may have been the happiest moment of her life. Then she felt a sudden cold sensation.

She came to with an ice pack on her neck, an oxygen mask covering her nose and mouth, and Ryan saying her name.

"You weren't a dream," she whispered, looking up at him, feeling overwhelmingly sleepy; wishing she could go back to being unconscious.

"You passed out.

"Listen, you want me to call Fitch's brother back here for you? Or maybe you want to call Glennis?"

Molly wondered for a second where she was and who Fitch's brother was, her thoughts returning very slowly to the present moment. "I want to go back to sleep," she said, remembering why she was there. Molly closed her eyes.

"Wake up, Molly." Ryan moved the cold pack to the other side of her neck and clamped something onto her finger. "This will monitor your oxygen levels."

Molly opened her eyes again. Would she ever see him smile again?

"Your cut isn't too deep. But passing out isn't good. You really should be seen by a doctor."

He fastened a scratchy, blue cuff onto her arm. It squeezed harder and harder, like loving the wrong person.

"Your blood pressure's ninety over fifty-one. That's low."

Molly heard what Ryan said but his voice sounded far like he'd stayed in the dream after she woke up. "Let me go back to sleep," she said.

"Molly," he said, in a firmer, less impersonal tone of voice. "You're too pale. I'm—"

Before Ryan could finish or Molly found the strength to say anything, Hugh and another tall, ropy man with earnest brown eyes crowded into the ambulance.

"It's just like you, Ryan, to sneak off and hide with the prettiest girl in the world," Fitch said, bending over Molly's leg. "How about an introduction?"

"Molly, Fitch. Fitch, Molly."

"Pleased to meet you, Molly."

Molly scowled.

"You feeling better, Molly?" Hugh asked.

"No," Molly said.

"Cut yourself pretty bad according to Hugh," Fitch said.

"I slowed the bleeding, dressed the wound. But she passed out," Ryan said.

Fitch turned to Hugh: "She always this pale?"

"No," Hugh and Ryan answered in unison, then glared at each other.

"You know her?" Fitch asked Ryan.

"Yes," Ryan answered, blushing.

"I see," said Fitch, with a genial air. "Are we taking you to the hospital or is my brother taking you to your doctor's office?"

Molly removed the oxygen mask.

"Not a good idea," Ryan said, approaching her to put the mask back on her face, but Molly sat up quickly, then stood, glowering at him. She shook the oxygen monitor off her finger.

"I want to leave—or at least talk to Ryan alone," she said.

Ryan and Fitch exchanged looks.

Molly didn't see spots this time. She did not see all three men reach out to catch her. This time, she just blacked out.

Days later, certain that Ryan wouldn't take her back, Molly had accepted the cemetery caretaker job and set out for Scarlet Maple.

6.

Molly's fever dream ended. Her eyelids flung open, revealing hazel irises surrounded by red webs. She swore she could still feel the cut oozing plasma. Hear the voices of men long gone from her life. She was supine on the couch with Annabel, sprawled out on her thighs, purring in her sleep. The vibrations soothed Molly's racing heart until it returned to stasis.

"Oh, sweetheart," she said, sliding her hand under the belly. Her legs and head slumped over her fingers.

"I'd hate to move you, but Momma's got some work to do."

Annabel remained on the couch, curling into a natal bliss. A stark opposite of the corpse of Mr. Nash.

The head slumped further down. The elbows bowing out on the armrests. The stench of blood and other fluids building, trying to escape. Molly surveyed it, wondering if her strength could even drag it. And just how far. The tombstones arrayed from the house like rays of the sun. That is how she would draw the sun in her childhood drawings. With long, thin rays, they'd wriggle out of the semicircle sun in the corner. Sometimes, the lines pierced the heads of the stick figure people. Their frolicking ceased by the graphite arrows.

She inhaled from her gut. She flexed her arms to get the circulation going.

"Here goes nothing," she said.

She edged her hands between the armpits. Underneath the flannel, the skin was tepid. Once she got the corpse into a full nelson, she lifted it. Her deltoids squeezed, pinching her. She grunted, shifting the torso upward until the legs handled some weight. Mr. Nash was not a tall man, nor hefty in stature, but a mold with organs and blood pooling at their lowest point. Once the torso cleared the armrests, she squatted on her trembling thighs. Despite all the commotion, Annabel still slept, unaware of the toils of reality.

"Cat can sleep through anything."

Molly's body burned as she dragged the corpse out onto the porch. It was the thick of night, with creatures roaming and buzzing about. Rustles through the bushes, and flutters through the trees. It was lively on that Georgian night. The first of many. She flicked on the porch light. Amber shrouding covered in cobwebs lit illuminated a few feet. Within seconds, mosquitos ambushed her. They darted around her in search of fresh, pumping blood. She felt the nibs on her neck, her arms. She turned the corpse and walked backward. She was panting. The boots hit every step. An ethereal gong in the night. She took a breather once she felt her own feet sink into the plush grass. The corpse followed. Nesting for the return to dust, it lay.

Molly regrouped on the steps, gazing out into the darkness. It was hard to focus on anything other than the corpse of Mr. Nash. Molly tried to count the wrinkles on the forehead. She pondered the acquisition of each one, making up scenarios in her head. Maybe Mr. Nash was first a mortician. Maybe he witnessed the aftermath of fatal car crashes. Of young teens overdosing on drugs. Of battered women & murdered gang members. He could have seen friends and family. Fled from the mortal coil faster than he could. Maybe, Molly thought, he regretted his position. Being the elderly guardian of thousands of dead souls. Maybe the wrinkles formed then, surrounded day by day by death, absorbing into him. Made him realize mortality was a privilege. The poetry he may have written, before that very night where he would write no more.

Now, it was seemingly her turn. To be the successor, she first had to bury the predecessor. She took in those same deep breaths and performed the same grasp.

"I hope I can find a plot for you, mister," she said.

She did not expect any protest, but the corpse did speak. A gurgling spewed forth from the mouth. It had the same intonation as Mr. Nash's voice on the phone. Gargled, weary. Weirdly, Molly felt at ease. It felt as close to a conversation as she could imagine. But if Mr. Nash was still speaking, still present in this world, she wanted his final opinion on where he wished to rest for eternity. They crossed into the column of graves, where the moonlight blanketed the land in a soft blue hue.

Then corpse began to spasm.

It started at the legs. Then the jolts reached the torso. Bucking from within the cavity of dead organs. The arms started to flail, and she gasped. She dropped the corpse and it writhed in the grass. She watched the fingers curl, excavating the soil. Rusty bile spewed from the mouth, soiling flannel and khakis. Then, as if a ghastly aura overtook the corpse, Molly watched the right arm lift and manipulate a single finger to point to a gravestone. HAMMERSMITH, it read. TO A SON, LOST TOO SOON.

Molly's lips trembled. "No, no way."

Her legs grew hot, and she ran. Into the depths of the graveyard, sprinting through thick grass, she stumbled over fallen branches and lawn-level grave markers. A cloud swallowed the moon. Tombstones appeared as jagged teeth in a black mouth of death.

"I gotta get outta here, I gotta get outta here," she panted.

She was lost among the dead. Wispy, melancholic beckons of spirits echoed in her ears as she ran.

"I'm sorry, I'm so fucking sorry," she screamed. She felt the hands of the dead pull at her clothes, her hair.

"Mama, why?" she heard over and over.

It was mania and it was real.

At last, she saw the pebbled road, then the waning porchlight in the distance. Her breath squeezed out of her diaphragm. She felt her abdomen absorb the knife in her waistband. She leapt over the last tombstone and felt the point drive into her thigh. She didn't land on her feet, tumbling into the road, dirt embedded into her arms and knees. She grasped her leg and winced in pain. The knife unveiled warm blood-streaked upon the blade The porch was a mere twenty yards. She rose with her weight on her healthy leg and hobbled. With adrenaline flooding her brain, she collapsed onto the stairs, crawling to the door. There was a red blotch growing on her jeans, waiting for her to get back to the confines to reveal its damage done. She crawled back over the threshold and kicked the door. It latched with a *thump*.

Annabel awoke in a panic. She fluffed her tail, arched its back, and emitted a curdling hiss.

"Shh, it's okay," Molly said. The pain in her leg arrived. "Fuck I need to wash this out."

She grasped the chair's velvet armrest and rose. She noticed the blood and plodded to the bathroom.

"Mama," a childish voice emitted from the house. Reverberated out of a void, encircling her.

Her face flushed in an instant while gazing into the mirror.

"Who? What?"

She heard Annabel hiss again. An invisible whirl of cool air enveloped Molly's body.

Then, a voice answered back, "It's time to repent, Molly Hammersmith."

7.

Molly Hammersmith hadn't heard her name.

She couldn't have.

Disembodied voices don't carry on icy breaths of wind, and icy breaths of wind can't make their way through a shut-tight house. Old dead men don't gurgle and puke themselves back to life, gravestones don't whisper. And one of those gravestones simply did not have Hammersmith chiseled into it.

The logic was sound. Simple. It was dark, she was dragging a corpse into a graveyard. She'd seen too many movies. Nothing to worry about aside from the bleeding knife wound in her leg, which was worse than it felt—the blotch of blood widening centimeter by centimeter as she stood on the bathroom's threshold, staring at Annabel staring, crossing her fingers so that non-existent wind doesn't crawl up her spine again.

Annabel cocked her head.

"I know, right?" Molly said.

Then Annabel's spine arched into a bell curve a moment before Molly was thrown into the bathroom.

Wall tile dusted her hair and shoulders, and chunks of the stuff tinkled to the floor. Pain radiated from her tailbone to the base of her skull and wouldn't allow her the mental energy to even attempt to explain this away. Nor would her clenched teeth or her strained breath hissing through her teeth.

But that was nothing.

She'd seen enough zombie movies to imagine the feeling of fingers tearing into a belly. How easily they pulled skin and muscle away once they got a good, firm grip on the sides of the split-open skin that begin with a single finger in a belly button. The feeling of staring into your own pulled-open body, watching your guts and liver and stomach come out with a wet *shluck*. All of it was proof you were already dead; your brain just hadn't caught up yet.

Molly's first grade teacher told her she had an overactive imagination.

Molly's first grade teacher was a fucking liar.

There was no zombie. No undead Mr. Nash. No Pet Sematary'd Annabel clawing into her gut. There was nothing but pain. Sharp, deep pain reaching into her, trying to open her up, crawl inside. Coiling, slithering energy shooting through her brain. Screaming, grabbing for whatever was doing this, she hoped her heart would give out from the pain before she had to watch her insides slide out of her, or her skullcap fall to the bathroom floor.

It took Molly much less time to figure out she wasn't coming to pieces than it felt like it should have. And each passing second in which she wasn't coming apart, she was able to take note of some details despite the hurt. There was a sense of desperation in the invisible force trying and seemingly failing to pull Molly open. Like its fingernails, if it had them, couldn't quite dig into her skin. Like its fingers (typically fingernails go along with fingers) didn't have the strength enough to do much more than cause superficial pain. Almost as if it needed not to fail and had little time left before it had to...

...let go?

She reached for her belly. Her hands came away with some sweat, a bit of lint from her shirt, but no sticky-wet blood or viscera. She massaged her temples, and ran her fingers through her hair, probing her skull. Again, nothing.

It didn't get in.

Couldn't.

She was still hurt. Bleeding from her leg. Pain in her back with each breath. But she was whole. There wasn't a time in her life when simply being in one piece was a baseline for personal wellness, but, depending on which way she would choose to look back on this later in life, maybe acknowledging previous good fortune in the face of shitty circumstances was the truer reference point regarding one's understanding of their station in life.

There would be plenty to think through later. And hopefully, plenty of time with which to do it. But now Molly needed to catch her breath, had to pull herself off the bathroom floor, and needed to get as far away from this place as possible.

Annabel, sitting, watching her from feet away, mewed, licked a paw, and looked at her with an indifference impressive for even a cat.

"Appreciate your help," she said.

Annabel opened her mouth to yawn.

Molly covered her gaping mouth with both hands.

The clicking and crunching of Annabel's pulled-open jaw turned Molly's stomach, but it was the sound the cat made from deep in its belly as something forced its way into its body through its mouth that bubbled the vomit into her mouth and down the front of her.

The cat, if she could even call it a cat anymore, morphed thrice its size. Its fur thinned across its expanding body, exposing the taught, overstretched skin beneath it. Lumps, like elbows or knees, ran this way, that, inside the thing that was Annabel. Cat bones, no longer anywhere near where they were supposed to be, drifted beneath the flesh until whatever it was inside...stopped. Like it was stuck. Had nowhere else to go, no space left to grow.

Molly reached for the knife, abandoned on the floor when she was thrown into the wall. She would step around whatever the thing that used to be Annabel was, knife ready to strike if need be. Once she'd made her way around it, she'd back away from the bathroom, keep her eyes on the thing on her way out the door just in case. But Molly wasn't able to take much more than a single step forward before grey, inhuman fingers found their way out of the cat's torn-open jaws. They trembled as if freezing now that they were exposed to the open air while searching for a proper grip.

Molly jammed the knife into what she could only describe as a cocoon—what her body would have been if that force had gotten in. The thing's arm unfolded itself and slapped her away.

Heat exploded from her hip as it glanced off the toilet. Her shoulder too once it collided with the clawfoot bathtub. Molly's body bounced off anything it touched from the force of whatever hit her.

There was no time for pain. No time for thought. No time for anything. She pulled herself to her knees, and crawled across broken tile and blood, feeling for the knife, bringing her eyes up to see if the thing was coming for her.

It wasn't coming for her.

But Molly was frozen in place, hands inches from the knife.

No, it was not coming for her.

But it was sitting, facing her.

Its arms wrapped around its knees. Its eyes—if they could be called eyes—were nothing more than distant glowing lights set dead-center in the deep black of empty sockets. A moan, deep and breathy but ending in a high-pitched whine, seeping from its lipless mouth in a golden mist that matched the color in its hollows-for-eyes.

"Jesus," Molly said.

The thing twitched.

It heard her.

It made a sound.

Throaty, deep. From somewhere in its chest.

Something like, "Jee."

And, "Siss."

"Jee-Siss."

Its breath coiled from its mouth like golden smoke every time it tried to speak. And now that it had gotten going, it wasn't stopping.

"Moll-Lee. Hamm-Merr-Smith."

And, "Miss-Ter Nehsh."

And, "Hannah-Bell."

The knife was again in Molly's hand, and before she even knew, plunged it into the side of the thing's head.

Maybe it was pain. Maybe rage. But the sound the thing made

as its mouth stretched to nearly the size of Molly's head made the broken tiles sing with the vibration. Made the floor shake. Made Molly's chest feel hollow as she used the vanity to vault over the thing.

The screaming continued as she sprinted through the house to the front door. As she yanked the door open. As she collided with someone just outside the light from the open door.

"Great Scott, Ms. Hammersmith," a familiar voice laughed. "You look like you got paid a visit from that spooky old raven from that one Simpsons episode way back when."

"Benchley," Molly said, panting, unable to pull air into her lungs. "We need to leave right now."

"Well hold up now, I just wanted to stop by because I feel like we got off on the wrong foot earlier—Christ on a bike, what's that unholy racket?"

The thing had stopped screaming by the time Molly had swung herself around.

But mimicking whatever she said—or seemingly thought—wasn't the only thing it could do anymore.

It was charging toward Molly and Benchley, legs shaky, feet unsteady, but making short work of the space between the bathroom and the front door. Benchley had unholstered his gun and was shouting all the things cops shout before they shoot at someone, but the thing's steps became more and more effortless. "Christ on bikes," it yelled, reaching out its massive arms.

"Christ on bikes," it screamed as its mouth stretched open wide.

"Christ on bikes," it said one last time before biting through most of Benchley's head.

Benchley got three shots off before the thing had him. Didn't matter. The gun thumped on the floorboards. Molly would have kicked herself for leaving it behind if she wasn't running as fast as she could.

8.

This fucking bitch, Benchley muttered while jimmying the ignition wires he yanked out of the steering column of Molly's SUV. The wires arced. The engine turned over, coughing into the night. Benchley rose and peered over the dash. The house was quite still. No sign of Molly coming. He killed the console lights, put the vehicle in reverse, and ghost rode slowly down the driveway—the tires crunched gravel like a steamroller over bones. At the main road, he put the transmission in drive and sped off a mile up the highway to where he left his police cruiser.

He slunk into the driver's side of the car and radioed his mom.

Did she call yet?

Not yet, a woman's voice said.

Let me know when she does.

He leaned back and lit a cigarette. *This fucking bitch,* he said again on an exhale, blowing the smoke into the ceiling of his car. *They never listen. They never fucking listen.*

He learned early on in his career that the rumors surrounding Scarlet Maple Cemetery had some weight to them. Mr. Nash had been dead a long time. Before Benchley was born. Before Benchley's mom and her grandma were born. Back when this whole part of the state was farmland as far as the eye could see.

Nash died while digging a grave and lay there for days before anyone came along. By the time they did the vultures had already torn open his pants and pecked at and ripped out his entrails through his anus. The long, blood-clotted intestines splayed out from him like casings in a sausage factory. The rest of his body fared no better. The cemetery cats had taken his eyes and lips. Nash had no kin, and the townspeople pushed the dirt on top of him. *Poor bastard dug his own grave* they thought.

It wasn't until later when the last of the carpetbaggers sent a surveyor down to look at the long-abandoned property that they found the piles of bones in an alcove behind a false wall in the basement. Bones too small to be an adult's. The town kept their secret. The house was forgotten until the visitors started showing up. Until the visitors began to disappear.

The radio crackled. *She called.*

And?

She's spooked.

Hopefully enough.

Be careful. Get her to leave.

Roger that.

Benchley flicked his cigarette onto the road. He knew he'd be there in a few minutes. He knew he'd put on his best gosh-golly-ma'am-my-apologies-my-momma-didn't-raise-me-like-that voice to get her to trust him. He knew he'd tell her he saw her car up the road. *Local kids foolin' around*, he'd rehearse. Then he'd play the role of concerned consoler and counselor. That he knew she came down here looking for a better future. *Your future is whatever you make it,* he'd say to the crying Molly. *So, make it a good one.* He knew he had to say whatever he could to get her away from the house if he wanted to keep his mom happy and uphold the oath he begrudgingly took.

He knew too many things that Molly didn't. But he didn't know that in a little more than a few minutes half his head would be ripped off, crushed between the jaws of a caul-covered Taltos—a clumsy newborn hungry for flesh. That the thing he was warned about would come to life on his watch.

**

Molly skidded out at the police cruiser. Her hands gripped the open door and then reached inside. *Please be there, please be there*, she said. And then, *Fuck,* as she felt an ignition naked of keys. She glanced back at the fiend, now hunched over Benchley. The taught sinews of its too-long extremities glistened in the moonlight. It dug its fingers into Benchley's head and scooped out the last of the sheriff's brain. It shoved its hand into the hole where a mouth would be and slurped down the goo. It raised its head to the moonlight and pulled off the slashed and torn caul from its face and body. It stretched its arms out and then held them in front like a praying mantis. It convulsed—joints cracking and snapping. A low gurgle came from its throat. A crescendo into an even, sonorous tone that radiated outward and vibrated the humid night air.

Molly felt panic leave her body.

A calm blossomed from her chest and spread throughout her limbs. The creature rose. It looked at Molly.

Momma...

9.

"Mama?" she said.

Her mother towered over her, drawing on a cigarette from one hand and holding the telephone receiver with the other. Her mother had two black eyes but neither one of them was what you'd think. Between bouts of drinking, she'd string together entire months of health: practicing a vegetarian diet, burning sage, balancing her chi. Crystals, acupuncture, Oregon grape essential oil. This time she was into kickboxing and accidentally got too close to her opponent, who kicked her right between the eyes.

Molly tugged on her pajamas. She could tell her mother was starting the slow slide into untouchable darkness. There was a bedroom at the back of the house where Darleen would begin to spend all morning, then all afternoon, until pretty soon she just wouldn't come out.

Four Roses, the bottle in her hand read. Molly could read now.

"What," her mother said, pulling the little hand away from her pants leg.

"Is Rod coming over?"

Her mother barked a laugh, and bent down to look Molly dead in the eyes, "Are you psychic, you little thing? That's who I'm trying to call."

Their windows were open and screened and faced the street. You weren't supposed to push on a screen; they looked strong, but they weren't. Hot, sticky air blew into the apartment, only to be swirled around by a box fan from Walmart. The apartment was small but at least it was cheap. Darleen could pay for it by herself, just from her post office job.

Things were always going wrong in the places they lived. First, there was the apartment with the leaking ceilings, so all three of them had to race around and carefully place pots underneath the drips. Then there was the Section 8 housing, which seemed nice at first (newly built!) but was later found to have been built with harmful materials. Darleen had blamed Molly's recurrent bloody nose on the drywall and laughed it off, but even back then Molly knew it was serious. She always took things more seriously than her mother. Why was that?

Now Darleen hung up the phone and sunk into the couch, immediately entranced by the TV. Molly sat quietly on the opposite side of the couch, slowly scooting closer and closer. Suddenly, a loud knock on the door. Darleen jumped to her feet and ran across the living room. She flung the door open wide and jumped into the man's arms. It was Rod, Molly could see. His wiry frame and old army coat. The two of them stumbled into the apartment as Darleen swung the bottle up so Rod could take a drink. Molly padded into the kitchen, found a jar of peanut butter, and took it to her room. She shut the door, locked it, and turned out the lights. Peanut butter tasted just fine in the dark, too.

**

"Mama?"

Molly snapped out of it. What the holy fuck was going on? The thing was facing her with its full attention now. She looked at her left hand, which was webbed between the third and fourth fingers, and back at the beast who had the same webbing on both hands. *My name is Molly Hammersmith. I'm 27 years old. I am having a panic attack. I'm not crazy. I'm not crazy.* Molly frantically tried to do the trick her therapist taught her, to ground herself by observing her five senses. I see my shoes, she thought. I hear my breath. I...I...

She hurled Dinty Moore cans from the counter, hurled them in a confusing assault, and sprinted to the front door. She ran through the woods, pawing at the brambles that seemed to grow not only from the ground up but also from the sky down. The air was soupy and cloying and every insect on the planet was fucking or dying or singing with joy. She ran and she ran and finally stopped to get her breath at the foot of a giant white oak that seemed to glow in the moonlight.

The wound was getting worse, or at least causing more pain. She tore her shirt and used it as a tourniquet. God, this was fucked. She snorted her grandmother's laugh, amazed at her strength. Up ahead she could make out the town's lights up and down the main street. And the football stadium lights on the edge of town were even closer. If she made it to town, she could hail someone down. It couldn't be that late, plus it was Friday.

Her progress slowed into hopping and resting, hopping and resting. The fields turned to a low-lying swamp, and she knew the wound could easily infect if it touched these waters and she might need to see a doctor. White rooms and needles. Molly pushed the thought away, but it was like the physical pain brought mental anguish. How she could have done what she did was beyond her now. It was like a different person committed that act. Maybe she was crazy then, or maybe she was crazy now, but either way, you looked at it, her life was divided by that one event. It happened and there was no going back. The child visited her in dreams, in different iterations. Sometimes it was a boy with curly dark hair, sometimes light-skinned or blonde or a little girl. She would start the dream holding the child, but invariably, she would lose it. She'd drop it or its head would snap back, or she'd lose it in a mall or some shit like that. One time she even said, "Not yet." What the fuck did that mean, *not yet?*

A road now. She climbed the steep embankment on her hands and knees and rested for a minute on the pavement. This would be much easier walking. She was going to make it. The tourniquet even seemed to be working. Headlights shone from behind and she put her hand out. The other one she put in her pocket.

10.

The headlights momentarily blinded Molly as the car pulled over to the side of the road. She vacillated between begging to be taken to a hospital--or anywhere far away from here--and pretending to be a harmless hitchhiker with connection to the horror she'd left behind at the cemetery. Whichever one was going to get her into the car faster. She didn't have a chance to speak before the driver leaned across the passenger seat and rolled down the window.

"Molly?"

She flinched and stumbled back. "Why do you know my name?"

"We spoke earlier," the woman said. "Now hurry up and get in."

Molly's body didn't quite feel entirely under her control, she managed to open the door and climb into the car. She hissed as the movement pulled at the wound on her leg.

The woman looked down at the blood-soaking Molly's jeans and then shifted into gear. Molly reached for the seat belt on autopilot, and fumbled with it, unable to get it to click.

"Don't worry about the belt."

They accelerated with a jolt back onto the road and Molly was slammed back into the seat. With regret, she let the seat belt go and it slithered back with a snap.

"My name's Ava."

"You're the operator," Molly said, finally putting the pieces together, recalling when she first picked up that phone, surrounded by the long-dead in their graves and the newly dead Mr. Nash, his cigarette still burning. "You welcomed me to Scarlet Maple before you knew why I was here."

"Why are you here?" She took a left turn so sharp that Molly's whole body tensed, waiting for the fishtail, but Ava's car kept to the road like a practiced caress. After a short distance of grooved pavement, the road turned to dirt with a bump that sent Molly sailing off her seat.

"I needed a job." Molly pressed the wound on her leg, the sickening pain stopping the confession from spilling out of her. Still, some truth needed to burst forth. "My grandmother told me not to come."

"I hope from now on, you'll listen to your elders."

Ava certainly was that. Wrinkled, liver-spotted hands held the steering wheel at the very top, fist against fist. Her hair was short and silver. It was pulled back with a silk handkerchief that might have been navy or deep green. She wore pearl stud earrings and something on a thick gold chain around her neck that hung low enough to sway across her abdomen. Hadn't Molly's grandmother always worn long pendants? Or was it just one, a locket or a pocket watch swinging as she walked? No matter how hard she tried, the memory slipped away from her.

The clouds that had been stealing what was left of the daylight. They let loose a band of rain, almost horizontal against the windshield. Molly wiped at her eyes as if that would clear away the blur, but they started to sting with the blood and dirt still on her hands. She wiped her palms on her thighs a few too many times in a row.

Another sharp left, this road pocked and uneven. The further they drove, the more potholes they hit until it was almost a rhythm. The lights of the main street of town were far behind and nothing had come to replace them.

"Where are we going?" Dirt roads lead somewhere, but that didn't mean it was somewhere good.

"You know how to use a gun?" Ava asked instead of answering. "Cast a spell? Draw a protective circle?"

Molly knew how to do one of those things.

"Not really," she said.

"Benchley." The name wavered as Ava spoke it.

Molly shook her head. She saw it again in fragments, the blood-soaked seat, the echo of when he'd called her young lady.

"We'll come back for him," Ava said, the drawl softened like she'd spoken that very phrase to herself many times before.

"Do you know what happened to Mr. Nash?"

"What happened to Nash was a long time ago."

"There's something back there," Molly said, and she shuddered hard, her skin breaking out into goosebumps.

"It knows you now," Ava said gravely. "It won't forget. That's why we need to get you safe."

Safe. When was the last time she had been safe? In Ryan's kitchen in the middle of the night, laughing with him as they ate cold pizza and drank warm beer? Under the cherry tree at her grandmother's house, birds singing outside in the overgrown wild rose bush, lilacs about to bloom? When her mother had drawn her a bath, adding drops of essential oils until everything smelled like sweet orange and cinnamon?

The voice that had told her the time had come for her to repent had sounded so familiar.

The road opens up into a wide, overgrown field and it takes Molly a moment to realize the reason she can see it is that it's lined by torches ahead.

Ava drops a hand from her tight grip on the steering wheel and clasps at the object hanging from the chain around her neck. She clutches it tightly and lifts it to her mouth almost as if she's about to kiss it. Her lips move but if she's actually saying anything, Molly can't make it out.

The torches flare, revealing a figure striding across the field.

"What is this place?"

Ava slows the car, then shifts it into park. "The beginning."

11.

The beginning was safe.

The beginning Molly remembered didn't include Ava or the eerie approaching figure; the remembered beginning lacked the cranked-up feel of a zombie quest.

It began in the *familiar* and *home-like*: two words that stared at each other across the small room of a child's mind. *Familiar,* as in the bath drawn by her mother, the waft of orange and cinnamon, the tenderness infused with uncertainty, the intimate closeness of association; *home-like,* as in the scent of canned food being reheated, the site which kept changing but served as a home, a place to which one could return.

There was the mother who lived in the land she invented from alcohol and loneliness; there was the poverty made inarticulable by a paucity of words. How to describe owning nothing when it resembled stacks of junk, piles of trash, a plethora of objects without value? If Molly forgave her mother, it was because language lacked words for so much lack: the staccato back-and-forth, the sparse dialogue, the love thinned by not knowing rich words for hunger, ruin, rot.

If Molly took things more seriously, it's because her mother's crystals had failed her. As a child, she'd witnessed the inarticulable seams: the magic meant nothing. There was no Mother Nature. No Gaia. No oil to improve their lives. There was no dead father; there was no ghost to whisper stories to her at night. Molly knew what she knew and said nothing: this was safer.

Safety was keeping silent when you saw what you shouldn't.

This, too, was familiar. Torches had lined the paths in her dreams. Although Ava and the figure weren't present, the scene was one she recognized. The fear was the new part: the terror was the alienated auspice of the girl who had been before and was now entering in someone else's tone.

Molly silenced the world for an instant, long enough to admit that the cemetery was the birthplace of everything she knew about herself. The cemetery was the beginning.

Familiar, as in a demon supposedly attending and obeying a witch, is often said to assume the form of an animal.

Familial, as in related to family, which included her grandmother's chickens and the dead father she never met.

Counter-spell, as in the therapist's tricks to distance Molly from the voices that knew things. The world worked at many levels, and it functioned most smoothly when those levels did not intersect. So, Molly could not be *herself* as long as she inhabited the whole. The therapist was paid to keep Molly hidden from herself, just as Ava was urging the same, in a worn voice that mapped over her grandmother's voice.

There was no place for Molly in this world her grandmother tried to keep at a distance.

There was a story between Ava and her grandmother that belonged to Molly, but it was a secret—and each secret kept her hidden from knowing herself. The beginning was safe; it was familiar; it included a cemetery: none of this was wrong or strange or dangerous.

The part that Molly needed to understand was why the beginning included *repentance*.

12.

Aside from sharing the story one time in a moment of overwhelming trepidation, Molly's grandmother Glennis planned on taking what she knew about the beginning to the grave. That was her idea of repentance: saving future generations from the torments she hid deep inside the recesses of her being. She, like Molly, had demons, making it feel like she was only partially in control of her life as if something else was pulling at the strings of her being.

The story had presented itself in vivid visions and fragmented dreams, which younger Glennis assumed were only that—dreams, intrusive thoughts—until she was old enough to know better until she was brave enough to search out the unnerving characters and eerie locations she saw whenever she closed her heavy eyes.

However, on the cusp of her fourteenth birthday, Glennis hadn't felt brave at all. After waking from a nightmare featuring a demonic black cat and a half-headed cop, she shared the narrative as she understood it with the petite girl tucked warmly inside a sleeping bag on the bedroom floor. Glennis's one and true companion in this world. Her best friend. Her dear, darling Ava.

Of course, Ava had promised Glennis that she wouldn't tell a soul. That whatever secrets best friends shared stayed between them. And while Ava had kept all her other promises—teenage crushes, first kisses—Ava couldn't hold this story in. The visions. The violence. And there was no going back after Glennis had let it loose. The story was out now, burning inside of them like swallowed matchsticks.

That next day, Glennis felt embarrassed about her overdramatic confession. All that terrible stuff was just her imagination, wasn't it? And she should have known she couldn't trust Ava with this. She couldn't trust anyone with thoughts as dark as these. But she did trust Ava. This is why Glennis was left completely baffled as to why Ava's father abruptly moved their entire family in the middle of the night as if they were fleeing something. Or, maybe, as if being pulled toward it.

**

"What is this place?" Molly asked Ava, who sat rigid as a corpse. Her hands gripped the steering wheel of the parked car.

Molly eyed the silhouette of a man, which seemed to grow taller as it walked toward the car from the torch-lined path.

"Ava, please," Molly pleaded.

"We'll need to talk to him first," Ava said.

"Who is *him*?" Molly screeched.

"The sheriff," said Ava.

"The sheriff? I thought Benchley was the sheriff."

"The Benchley you knew was the deputy sheriff. A shithead if you ask me, God rest his soul. This is another Benchley. His father. My brother, Amon."

At that, the figure tapped on Ava's window.

"Let's go," the figure said, his voice hollow from outside the car.

**

Inside an old chapel, lit only by candlelight, Molly pieced together the story as best as she could.

From her understanding of what the rambling sheriff shared, it started with a man named Clarence Nash, who was bequeathed the family business after his father died suddenly at the age of 38.

"It goes like this," Amon Benchley said. "It's a dark and grievous year. Nineteen hundred something. I see it play out like an old film. Black and white. Grainy. And there's a boy. He's 16 years old, but he quickly transitions from Little Clarence the teenager to a bold Mr. Nash in no time. At first, the townspeople respect how quickly and how seamlessly he takes on the role of caretaker. And taking care he did.

"Under young Mr. Nash's proprietorship, Scarlet Maple Cemetery bloomed like never before. Within months of his father's passing—"

"I'm sorry" Molly interrupted. "But you sound more like an English professor than a sheriff."

"Amon is an eccentric man, but a brave man," Ava said. "The two can coexist, you know. Now, let's not be rude. There's a lot to learn and too little time as it is."

Ava made a motion with her hand as if to say, *Go on, continue.*

"Yes. Where was I? So, this Mr. Nash. He's 16. Head caretaker. An able young fellow. Touching up the paint on the gate, planting purple beds of chicory and bachelor's button. But he couldn't do everything alone, so he hired an acquaintance of his named Herman Hammersmith to help with the bookkeeping."

"Hammersmith?" Molly yelped.

"Molly, please," Ava said. "Listen."

Amon went on.

"Years passed. Business was booming. Which, in the grand scheme of things, illustrated dire circumstances in the area. Tuberculosis, cholera, typhoid fever. But things changed all of sudden. Something shifted. Not in terms of the dying, but where the townsfolk were being laid to rest. Despite the increase in mortality rates, fewer plots were being purchased at Scarlet Maple Cemetery.

"It wasn't until late one evening at the local drinking hole when Mr. Nash found out why his business was declining. That night, he was approached by a group of hecklers. Men he knew but men he avoided. And it quickly became clear to him. Gossip had pinned Mr. Nash as a nancy, and the men wanted to make their stance known. It was why folks were choosing to bury their kin outside of Scarlet Maple. It was why the men became violent."

Molly wanted to speak again, to interrupt the story—no, more than the story. She wanted to jump into the past and protect the man who she had only seen as a corpse.

Amon continued.

"For two days, Herman Hammersmith nursed Clarence's battered body with frozen venison and fed him small droplets of dark, soothing syrup. But that third night, Herman made it clear, that he had to relocate, that he had to break it off with Clarence. He said it was about time for him to find a wife. Start a family.

"From what I know, you didn't get to meet Mr. Nash, did you, Molly? If you did, you would have right away pinned him as a linguist. He had this poetic way of speaking. For him to plead with Herman would have sounded like this: 'My love, my joy, my everlasting. I will die. I will drag my already dead body out in the graveyard and dig myself the only home imaginable in a world without you.'"

Molly let loose a small giggle, but she was the only one to laugh.

"Herman, on the other hand," Amon said, "I imagine him as something different. Brutish. And he wasn't willing to stick around and die for love. Frankly, I think he feared dying at the hands of the townspeople. We're all afraid of dying, aren't we? And though he had surrounded himself with death for quite some time at the cemetery, the violence Mr. Nash experienced made it too personal, too close. And once Mr. Nash was healed enough to take care of himself again, Herman made plans to leave.

"Night came and Herman kept his word, leaving Mr. Nash alone at Scarlet Marple. And when Mr. Nash woke in the morning, Herman's stuff was gone except one thing: a small and shiny pennant on the table."

Molly waited for more, but the pennant seemed to end the story. A heavy silence hung in the chapel-like a spirit. And the newness of the quiet made the room feel even colder. Molly's hands felt like rusty steel. She wanted to leave the claustrophobic chapel and warm her bones by the pile of wood begging to be lit by one of the many surrounding torches.

"I don't understand," Molly said. "How was my grandmother involved in this? And how are the two of you? How am I?"

"Your grandmother is on her way here as we speak. It's the

only way we can put this whole thing to rest," Ava said.

"But why? I don't understand. None of this makes sense."

"Consider the story of Mr. Nash a prologue," Amon said, standing now, pacing around the rotten pews. "The real beginning starts here, at this chapel. Where Herman first came after leaving Mr. Nash."

Amon stopped in the center aisle and stared upward. "Each story has a beginning and an end, but you have to realize, that beginnings are subjective. Every person starts somewhere different. But the ending, that's where everything comes together."

"Then let's get on with it. Whatever we have to do," Molly cried. "I want this to end right *now*."

"Honey, I'm so sorry," Ava said, gently placing a hand on Molly's knee, avoiding the dark stain of blood. "There's still a lot we have to do. But for now, we wait for your grandmother. My dear old friend Glennis, whose life I ruined by sharing her secret with the wrong people."

13.

The lights of oncoming traffic cut jagged silhouettes around the highway dividers. Glennis Hammersmith had purchased the Greyhound ticket a few days ago to see her granddaughter in Georgia when she'd received a message on her answering machine from a woman claiming to be Ava.

Ava. It was a name that Glennis remembered well, despite the negative space between their lives now spanning sixty-odd years. They say the mind and body are hardened, like cement, into their final form as early as thirteen—that the bulk of life's shaping influences has already been felt, their damages or gifts already planted for future harvest. Ava had lived on in Glennis's mind for all this time, the few intense years of their bright friendship cut short by betrayal and sudden absence as Ava and her family had moved away without notice once Glennis had revealed hidden truths. Despite being able to trace back to that point the unraveling of her own life, it was a gap so keenly felt to that day that Glennis—upon hearing the voice of this old woman claiming to be her estranged childhood friend—staggered back from the machine as though it contained within itself an ancient ghost. Her throat tightened as she sat on the floor by the doily-laced window, listening to the message. Ava knew she'd ruined everything but still begged Glennis to come to Georgia to see Molly, to set things right. Her voice was strained as she spoke, as though she held dark secrets just beneath the tongue, waiting for them to be spoken by some unseen force.

The Greyhound driver honked. Glennis gripped the plaid fabric of the bus seat as the vehicle shuddered to a stop. Ahead, above the sea of other seats and curious passengers angling for a better view, Glennis could see a string of red brake lights. She heard the driver mutter the word "Fuck" and settle back into his seat to wait.

The rain had begun to fall gently. Glennis listened to it beat its rhythm into the bus's metal casing as they sat there in the dark, each face around her hidden by shadow, a stranger forever as though predetermined by something far off and intangible. A world full of strangers, she thought.

To her left, she saw something indistinct moving by the tree line on the opposite side of the road—surely an animal of some kind, perhaps a deer. It was hard to tell through the growing rain but as it moved, it became clear that it was not an animal but a person, a man of indeterminate age. The man was rail-thin; he hobbled across the double-lane highway, pausing for a moment on the cement path separating the two sides of the road. In the passing headlights, Glennis thought he looked like a soldier of some kind and was reminded of her own dearly departed Bill. They'd brought him back from the War a changed man, emaciated and wounded heavily. They were still working out the precise details of what had happened when she went to see Bill in the Army hospital. She'd passed room after room of mangled bodies on her way to him, each barely older than a child and torn apart by bullets and knives and bombs and landmines. She dragged Darleen, barely four, through the antiseptic halls, shielding her eyes as best she could from the possibility of seeing appendages and limbs missing, bones crushed to powder. When she'd gotten to Bill's room she cried. They told her he had weighed just ninety pounds when they found him and had been severely ill with malaria and beriberi. Some of his fellow soldiers had spoon-fed him until he was at least well enough to be transported back to America, but his mind was gone. The damage seemed to them irreparable, and the wound it tore into Glennis would never be healed. He was unresponsive, but still, Glennis stayed with him— had sent Darleen to be with her cousins—until he'd gasped to some sort of life. Looked at her intently as though she were a stranger.

"Mama," he said.

"My mother is a fish," he said.

And then he died. And everything changed again.

The figure outside rapped bony knuckles against the bus door. All of Glennis seized into a tight knot as the driver reached for the door mechanism. "Don't open it," she whispered, but it was too late. Into the bus wafted the familiar scent of blood and ash. With sudden vivid clarity, Glennis recalled from her childhood this exact scent, was transported on it to another time, into another body, another Glennis from long ago. This was the figure from her dreams who had spoken to her in whispered singsong cadence, had told her of some great calamity. The dreams had taken such a toll on her that, in desperation, she'd found at the library a copy of the *Diagnostic and Statistical Manual of Mental Disorders*, but when she'd looked up conditions associated with hallucinations, the answers all frightened her: Alzheimer's, dementia, encroaching blindness, macular degeneration, delirium, Creutzfeldt-Jakob disease, epilepsy, schizophrenia, brain tumors. The thought of her body hosting any or all of these things had made her palms sweat and she'd closed the book with a solid thump as if to say *no*, as though that would help.

The bus driver turned the lights on towards the front of the bus. "Can I help you, man?"

The yellow lights shone down directly over the figure's head, casting its face in shadow, but Glennis recognized it immediately. Though Glennis alone seemed to recognize this, its face was stitched together like a baseball's cowhide exterior: jagged slivers of all different faces, each recognizably human but distinct from one another. The figure turned from the driver to the aisle and settled its shoulders solemnly. As though in recognition of some necessary action it did not want to do. Like Jesus setting his face to go to Jerusalem. She thought of the Yeats poem from long ago: *And what rough beast, its hour come round at last, / Slouches toward Bethlehem to be born?*

The figure stepped towards her down the aisle. Glennis tried her best to move into the fabric of the seat beneath and behind her, gripping the seams with impassioned fear. Her ears rang, a familiar sound from the dreams of long ago, and she felt as though she were being reborn, a flightless bird being given new wings. Felt as though she could do anything, could turn back time, go to the beginning of all this, fully embody herself as she'd been then, redo it all but better this time. She could stop Bill from going to war, stop him from dying; and even if she couldn't, she could fill herself with more love, whisper the things to herself that she needed to hear, things that could change everything. She could be more present with Darleen, not worry so much about the future, and enjoy what they had.

She heard the sound of wet footsteps as the beast, rain dripping onto the aisle, approached. "If you play stupid games, you'll always win stupid prizes." She said this to someone but was no longer sure who. There was a ringing in her ears. She no longer knew where the sound was coming from.

14.

Somewhere in the distance—it could have been a hundred miles away or less than 20, as time and space always moved differently when one was on the Greyhound—Molly was eating eggs and drinking coffee, her first hot meal in who-could-remember-when. Was it morning or the middle of the night? Who could say at this point? Certainly not Molly.

Ava was watching Molly, looking for Glennis in her movements. Sometimes she could see it in how she held the cup, titled ever so slightly forward. Or when Molly looked at Ava as if she was looking through her, just like Glennis had when they would play pretend. Then it was gone again.

Together, they waited and did not discuss the ominous feeling they each had – the feeling that made Molly's hair stand up on the back of her neck and made Ava feel like a child again, back in that bedroom, Glennis's voice like something she'd never heard before and had hoped to never hear again.

**

Hammersmith, the creature said without speaking as it took the spot beside Glennis.

She nodded to the back of the bus seat.

It was a conversation she had been waiting on for decades now. Her fingers picked at the siding of her seat as if they were not of her body anymore – as if she was just an old woman on the last leg of the trip to see her granddaughter. It could have been so simple if things had just been different.

The creature—the man? The thing? Whatever it was, it laid its appendages that looked like hands on her knee. They were as if the features of hands had been there once but were long gone now, erased by time. They were neither cold nor warm. Glennis could barely feel the weight of the hands-that-were-not through her pants.

Then it pressed down harder, and she could feel everything at once. She had to bite her tongue to stop her scream. The blood tasted of rusted pennies and her tongue, like raw meat.

**

She had seen what happened to women who screamed. She had tried to teach it to Darlene and later Molly.

"Do not be afraid of the pain," she had told them each as children. It had been different decades, but both mother and daughter had a wild streak in them. They had both climbed trees only to fall from them, both found themselves busted up after ill-chosen fights, both chased chickens through the same hen house outside, and had both been pecked until they had bled. Darlene, it had been her hand, on a cold morning in her childhood. Molly, her thigh, on the hottest day of summer. Both of their blood had spilled into the dirt and disappeared as if it had been sucked back into the hungry earth.

When Glennis had heard them scream, she had tended to their wounds, of course. She kissed knees on very rare occasions but more often had run the cuts and scrapes under cold water and bandaged them up without ceremony, less they think there was some kind of pageantry in their pain. She had reminded them both, time and time again, "If this was the worst thing that ever happened to you, then you've had a pretty damn good life."

It was implied: And for the love of God, don't scream next time. Or ever if you can help yourself.

And eventually, they learned to stop screaming too.

It was an inheritance—to swallow the pain. Let it chew against your guts before you let it out. You had to be stronger or better or faster than the pain because it would kill you if you let it. It had tried with Glennis before, and she knew it would try with all her daughters, and their daughters, and their daughters. This was their penance, for the sins of their forefathers. Or perhaps, just the one forefather.

Darlene had muffled it with alcohol, with that damned husband of hers, with the kickboxing and dieting and crystals and things Glennis couldn't bear to think of her only daughter doing. She had always been sensitive, her Darlene. The nightmares were too much for her.

Molly was tough. She had tried to correct the wrong of her mother and instead of pushing it inside, she wore the pain like armor. She was strong like Bill was before the war. Like Glennis's own mother, a mountain woman who had dropped out of school in eighth grade but could sense if someone was pregnant and what they were carrying before they could. Even the chickens had been afraid of her.

She had married a traveling man from Georgia, Glennis's father by all accounts. She had reared him two daughters before and when she told him there would be a third, he up and left without so much as packing a suitcase. That was the version Glennis was told, and she had never openly questioned it. Or at least, certainly not to her mother. After that night with Ava, she had been reminded that her power was in her silence. Talking about it was all too painful for everyone involved.

**

Back on the Greyhound, blood mixed with spit dripped down her chin. A well had sprung from her nose, but she didn't dare move to wipe it.

She tried to focus on the sounds of the man snoring three seats up, but it had long since faded into the damned ringing. Her body vibrated as if to try and match the pitch.

Hammersmith, the creature said again, pushing down harder, and tears cracked through her eyes. Her mouth twisted back and forth, a wild creature she couldn't tame for much longer. The creature seemed to smile.

The blood rolled down Glennis's skin, down the curve of her face, down past her lips which had finally been cracked apart, down as Glennis took in a deep breath to ready her body, down through the moist air of the greyhound until it landed on the hands-that-were-not and the creature recoiled, yanking its body back into itself.

Glennis doubled over, her hands covering her mouth.

Wrong one, the creature said, and for the first time, she looked into its eyes – if you could call them that.

This wasn't how things were supposed to be. Something was wrong. The creature was already moving back down the aisle, and the ringing was getting softer.

The greyhound came to a sudden stop, and Glennis stood with a lurch. She pressed her hands, bloodied red, into the back of the seat to steady herself and tried to remember how to breathe. When she had her footing, she rummaged in her pocket for a handkerchief and wiped the blood from her face. She needed to look at least semi-presentable for the occasion, after all.

It was her stop.

15.

Molly stumbled onto the sidewalk, leaning on the diner door's faded lacquer. Almost a pot and a half of coffee sloshed with each step, and one kind of fullness made up for another emptiness. The dull throb of her leg made up for that, too. So many losses, but a good diner breakfast, at any time of the day, was a win.

The soft shuffle of Ava's tennis shoes joined her at the curb. From between the buttons of her oversized cardigan, a blue glimmer. "That pendant, Ava, is that a sapphire?"

"Oh yes, a family heirloom. Family protection."

"It's the mother-stone…"

"Yes, darlin'. But you have to keep it tucked away in this moonlight. Who knows what it might pick up with that fullness?"

Ava nodded towards the sky, but all Molly saw were clouds backlit by something that felt larger than the sun. Through this celestial veil, it was a warm spotlight.

"One more stop before Glennis."

**

Whatever the meal and wound had dulled, the fluorescent lights of the gas station pierced. A leather strap of Christmas bells atop the door heralded their entry. In Molly's childhood, there were years of Slurpees and hot dogs, and years of brown rice and broccoli sprouts. The hot dog years were the good ones.

"Three shakers of salt! Then I'll get the rest," Ava said.

Molly wandered towards the condiments as Ava headed towards household supplies. She had one hand around a limp and empty canvas bag. The other hand raised the pendant to her ear. Ava made a sharp turn in another direction, nodded, and picked up a lighter.

"You sure?" she breathed to an imaginary listener. She

replaced the lighter with a box of matches.

"You're right. Much better."

**

Eccentricities are part of aging. Or you're born with them. Or brought up with them. Darleen would talk to her crystals, sometimes even sing as she lined them up on the windowsill the night before a full moon. "Time to charge! Without these, *the ce-en-ter can-not ho-oh-oh-old*." Old poems as songs. Stones as friends. Molly would line up the beer bottle caps next to them, to see if her mother would notice. Little villages of wine corks like purple-topped sentinels. "*Mere an-nar-chy*," Darleen crooned. "This is how we keep safe." For Molly's thirteenth birthday, a smooth disc of carnelian. "It's flat so you can keep it in your bra! Just in case." She winked.

And then only four years later, Molly would line her rocks on bedroom windowsills, fished out of strangers' sheets, plaid flannels, and sweet florals with scalloped edges. "*Can-not ho-oh-oh-old*," she found herself crooning, and would explain it as a rare Beatles' B-Side. "Come back to bed, baby," they'd inevitably say. And she would, lifting the top sheet like a veil, between webbed fingers.

**

Finally, the right aisle. Molly grabs the cardboard salt & pepper shakers. Three pairs worth in the crook of her elbow. It seemed like a waste if they wouldn't use the pepper but who knows? If Ava was listening to a divine recipe, they probably had a proclivity for the spicy.

Spice it up.

Molly let out a laugh only to herself. She spun on a heel to the shelf behind her. Cat food. Tiny tins with printed cartoon fish. Ava noticed her lingering and came over. Her bag held future necessities already.

"Be careful of the strays, Moll. Once they get any sense of

affection, you're stuck with them for life. Either yours or theirs."

Annabel another type of orphan back at the Nash house. A splatter like strawberry jam. Bones like pretzel rods. Egg-skull.

"Right," Molly said.

She left the food aisle and ventured to the back of the store. Walls of cans and bottles, glass, aluminum, and so many iterations of the same thing. Her hand trailed across the cool, smooth refrigerator doors. Then, on the adjacent wall, more coffee. The warmth from the diner, from Ava. Too comfortable meant too careless. She let her fingers dance on the speckled counter, around the metal edge of the burner.

Caution: Hot.

It sounded like a challenge. Or a test. Would she remember if it came to that? To be the one who doesn't scream? She held her palm next to the half-empty carafe.

I am not a woman who screams.

A mantra from Darleen, some ancestral maternal wisdom.

I bet I can do five whole seconds.

Molly took a deep breath.

One...two...three...

"Let's go, darlin'!"

Ava's shrill call pulled from her trance. Her hand tingled, barely singed, but ached with a familiar awakening.

I could have done all five without a peep. Maybe even ten.

At the counter, Ava had lined up one box of matches, one bottle of lighter fluid, three tubes of lipstick in varying shades of red, a bottle of aspirin, two tree-shaped air fresheners, and a bag of marshmallows.

"Anything else?"

The cashier's automatic, halting drawl turned sweet.

"Hun?"

She was not unlike Molly. Probably the same age, but without the webbed fingers. As was Molly but without a protruding belly. She guessed seven months along.

"Get yourself a treat, just in case," Ava said. The total on the screen kept rising. She was indulgent.

Comfort from whatever was to come. Molly scanned the row of candy bars, eye level for a kindergartener.

Was each nicety a type of intergenerational apology? What had *happened between her and grandmother?*

Molly picked a Baby Ruth. The most nutritionally dense, according to Darleen.

Ava continued her order. "Two cases of .22s, and one .38s. And a pack of menthols."

"Smoking is bad for you," Molly said. It was Darleen's voice escaping from her own throat.

As if bullets aren't.

"They're for Mr. Nash. Add it to my tab, Angel."

The cashier winked and pointed at Ava with a finger-gun click. Ava opened the sagging canvas tote at her side and with the expert gesture of one hollow-boned arm. The weight of the bounty swung into Molly's injured leg. She winced and all her memories dissipated. Across the street, a Greyhound bus sputtered to a stop. Somewhere else, a man with seven faces dragged himself across the South. And somewhere familiar, over the remains of Benchley Jr., someone else waited for Mama.

16.

Molly felt something wet at her upper lip and dabbed the bit of blood leaking from her nose, making sure Ava wouldn't notice. As a child, she'd gotten nosebleeds quite often and her mother always blamed the dry air of Kentucky. Deep down, Molly knew that wasn't the reason why, though she'd never be able to express it back then.

"You alright, hon?" asked Ava, who noticed Molly's sudden malaise. Glennis slept in the seat beside them, exhausted from the pain of silence on another Greyhound. They were on a different bus now, en route through the woods to yet another distant and undisclosed location; one further down the path marked by death and ash.

Molly nodded out of what seemed to be compliance. "Yeah, just thinking."

The haunting image of Mr. Nash in that chair crept up her esophagus again. She placed her webbed hand on her stomach and stuffed the bloody napkin into her pocket with the other.

"I thought Nash died?" she said bluntly.

Ava fiddled with the supplies on her lap and smiled. "What exactly *is* death, my darlin'?"

Molly thought about all of the dead things she'd seen in her life: the chickens, her father, Benchley. Even the gravestones atop people she'd never meet. All of it sunk into her soul like centuries of temporal symbiosis.

She shrugged. "I dunno. The end of the road?"

"Now, if I were to suggest that the end of one road is simply the beginning of another, would you believe me?"

"If we were talking about *actual roads*, sure. What's that got to do with dying?"

"Roads have many travelers...from all walks o' life, Moll. Some are simply along for the ride while others like to drive. We all take part in both, at some point or 'nother." Ava glanced out the bus window and let the darkness of night soak her words. "Surely y'all heard the proverb: It's not the destination, but the journey that counts for sumthin'! That's how it be." She turned back to Molly and smiled. "Drivin', ya see, is a skill that can be taught but only *truly* learned through experience."

"I don't follow. What's this got to do with Mr. Nash? Where are we going?"

"There are things about this world that nun-yah understands, deary. One is the transition from livin' to dyin'." Ava looked over at the slumbering Glennis and then said, "Drivin' along roads with a map is one thing, sweetie, but using those roads that Frost was talkin' about the ones less traveled. Those are like the very one we're moving about right now."

"So, what are you saying?"

"Oh, for heavens! You're a smart gal, Moll, you know exactly what I'm saying: the road between livin' and dyin' goes in two directions. And drivin' either way is sumthin' to be learned! Don't you see? It makes all the difference."

Molly knew just like she knew about her nosebleeds. The prizes were always connected. The games were all headed in the same stupid direction. And at this junction of her life, she was yet again unable to express her deep wisdom of resurrection. Ava knew this too. So did Glennis. The only difference between the three of them was webbed hands and memory circuits lost to time and trauma. Generations of power coated in rust.

"We've got a long ride, my dear, why don't you try to get some rest?"

Molly nodded again and leaned against the cool glass of the window. Its comfort helped her close her eyes. Through all of this, Ava had become a spirit guide. Molly's shaman. There'd be nothing at the end of this road without her. She felt an immense rush of gratitude as she dozed off, letting the dim lights of traffic and night sky caress her mind to rest. For the first time in a long time, she felt momentarily safe.

Ava mumbled apotropaic spells to herself while her companions slept. She focused on trying to avert the evil eyes of the higher spirit, knowing that it was frivolous at this point. Annabel was no spirit. Annabel was above time. The possession over that cat came from the same realm that caused Molly's nosebleeds. Ava knew she'd have much to teach Molly before facing the belly of the whale. Determination was there, but it would take some unlearning for Molly to understand her role in all of this. Metamorphosis isn't easy for anyone, let alone deities born to egregious amnesia and grave circumstance.

"How is she?" asked a sleepy-eyed Glennis.

Ava looked across the aisle; "Oh, she's beginnin' to realize," she said. "We mustn't let her see the truth 'til she's ready. It'll destroy her."

"You're right about that, dear friend." Glennis glanced out the window, still opaque with darkness. "Are we going where I think we're going?" she asked.

"Do you have any better ideas?"

"I suppose not. Does she know of its origins yet?"

"She knows only what she saw."

"Have the nosebleeds returned?"

"Unfortunately, so," nodded Ava. "We're running out of time."

Glennis chuckled. "You told me that time is a road without end. You know the circular nature of this beast." She looked at Molly, asleep against the window. "She is strong. Like us. We must keep our faith. The prophecy has yet to be wrong so far."

Ava sat up straight in her seat. "That's the part I'm 'fraid of, my darlin'."

"I'm sorry about your brother." She placed her hand on Ava's and smiled. "We'll find him soon enough."

17.

The greyhound was loaded with that early morning static that discharges with the sunrise. Molly stirred, her mouth felt sour, she tried to swallow the taste away but a lump in her throat stopped it from going down. She stood up, it felt good to stand, and she looked out the windshield. They drove down a black road in the dark, the only thing distinguishing the ground from the sky being the glowing white stripes the bus kept itself between. She felt like she was riding in a slot car.

Molly sat back down and dozed off again. She dozed off a dozen times, each time waking up to the morning dark. She wasn't sure when she started smelling gasoline, but she knew she smelled a lot of it. She wanted to ask Glennis if she smelled it, too, but the bus seat felt too much like a hug. She couldn't help herself from slipping back off into sleep.

She woke up smelling sulfur, with the feeling of great big lights behind her. Reds and yellows and blues. She woke up to hollering, and she kept falling back asleep.

It pulled right up next to the greyhound and with the collective throttle explosion of sixteen choppers, Molly woke and stayed awake. They swarmed the bus, they launched fireworks at the windows, they whipped a mirror off with chains, and they cut at the tires with saw-tooth machetes. From the inside of the bus, it felt like they were passing through an incinerator car wash.

A rider took point in front of the bus and forced the greyhound to stop.

Molly turned to wake Ava and Glennis, they were already awake, eyes narrowed, mumbling secret prayers into their hands. "What's going on?"

A shrill megaphone cut through any thoughts Molly could have had. "Well, now. Hello there folks. I don't want to waste too much of you good folks' time, so we'll get right to it. My name is Rufus Stillborne, hello, and this is my gang of mutant biker miscarriages. Now, say hello, gang."

With varying degrees of success, the gang said hello to the bus. Molly tried looking out the window, but Glennis squeezed her knee. "Don't."

Rufus continued his announcement. "Now, this will only take a minute, but we need everyone off that big ole' bus. Come on, everyone off the bus."

One by one, the passengers filtered out. Ava leaned over Molly, talking right at Glennis. "We need to get her out of here."

"We can't, they got us all locked up."

"Well...what are we supposed to do?"

Rufus continued, a bit more agitated, "Come on, folks, I said off the bus. We need you off this big ole' bus, now."

Glennis stood up. "Looks like we'll have to get off the bus."

"They'll spot her."

"Molly, you got a gun, right?"

Molly nodded.

Glennis brandished a gun of her own. "Listen, play it straight, do what they say and when I make my move you hop on a bike and you keep on heading down this road, alright?"

Rufus eyed the seated women. "I see you three holding up the line, now don't you make us come up there, come on now, off the bus."

"What about you two?" said Molly.

"Don't worry about us, we'll run into each other one way or another."

Rufus held the horn on. "Hey! I said get! Get off the damn bus!"

Sandwiched between her relatives, Molly walked off the bus. A biker dressed in all black leather met them outside.

"Howdy, I'm Slint, now you three little missies can come with me." He held onto each of their hands and guided them to the line of passengers.

Something struck Molly. She felt as though there was something off with Slint. Maybe it was the cologne he was wearing? Or maybe it was the bright green hair that sprouted out of his head. It took her a moment to realize that she, Ava, and Glennis were each holding on to a different one of Slint's hands.

Slint turned to Ava. "Oh, you're a frisky one. You better keep those little hands to yourself."

Ava flinched her hand back and stuck something in her pocket.

He put them in a spot between two other groups. "Now, you three stay right there. Rufus will be here in a second to eye you all down." Then, he went back to the bus to guide more passengers along.

Molly looked at Glennis.

Glennis looked back. "They work for Nash."

"But why are they so—"

A motor-trike rolled up to them. "Why so what, sugar?" Rufus stopped in front of Molly. "Why are we all so handsome? Well, that's a hard one to answer. Some say it's cause of the bikes." He revved up his trike. "But I like to think we have some sorta unnatural charm that makes us just..." He licked his hand and slicked back his hair, "Eerie-Istable." He stuck out a hand to Molly, "Rufus Stillborne, pleased to meet ya!"

Molly was speechless at the sight of Rufus. He was a gruff guy, all red and sweaty, barrel-chested. He had a long black beard and a big bushy eyebrow, but that wasn't what struck Molly. What struck her was how his motor-trike looked a little bit like a baby carriage, the fact that his massive torso was connected to toddler legs, and what shocked her the most was the massive single eyeball in the center of his face.

Rufus grabbed Molly's hand and shook it hard. "Well, hell, it's nice to meet you, kid! Actually, now that I'm thinkin' 'bout it, you look kinda fra-mrilliar. You wouldn't happen to be..." And Rufus pointed his massive eye at Ava, then Glennis. "Well, gee-shit. You wouldn't happen to be that little squirt Molly we been hearing so much about, would ya?"

Molly slid her hand out of his grip, she backed away.

Rufus lit off a bottle rocket. "Yeeeee-haaaaw! Boys and girls gather round, we have found ourselves our little Molly!" and he went on hootin' and hollerin' like a big Texas cowboy. "Woooweee! Folks, you are free to get back on the bus, have yourselves a nice little trip, goodbye, farewell, bomb boy-age, we got our girl!"

The other passengers marched back on, but the bus did not drive away on account of the flat tires.

The other bikers zoomed over and drove in circles around Molly, Ava, and Glennis. Each one of the bikers had an odd number of eyes, arms, and mouths. Each one of them lit off enough fireworks to put a new sun in the sky.

Molly wanted to run, she wanted to fly but there was nowhere to fly to, so she just stomped around like a startled raccoon. The two old women stood still and waited for the show to stop.

With a wet fingered whistle, Rufus brought the show to a stop. "Alright, alright, enough horsing around. Grab them—"

But before the words could leave his mouth, Glennis drew her pistol.

Molly's ears rang, she smelled sulfur again, and before the smoke cleared Glennis was down bleeding on the pavement.

Rufus tucked his six-shooter into his pants. "This isn't my first time around that never-ending road, Glenny."

Molly crouched down next to Glennis. "Grandma—"

She shushed her. "Take this," she said, handing Molly her necklace. "Don't worry, you'll see me again, soon." Then, with a cough, she was gone.

Ava helped Molly up and the two held each other.

Molly felt tears burn down her face. "What are we going to do?"

She heard a match strike, a fuse burn.

"We stick to the plan," Ava said.

"Is that crying I hear?" said Rufus. "Enough of that, come on, time to—"

The bottle rocket Ava was aiming went off. A screamer squealed past Molly's ear and exploded into a meaty pupil.

"Ah! Fucking dammit. My big ole' fucking eye!" Rufus held his face. "Ah, what the fuck! Get those fucking fuckers dammit!"

Before the bikers could rush them, Ava and Molly whipped out their pistols and picked a few of them off. They fell to the ground screaming as their bikes ran wild circles around them.

Rufus reached for his gun and shot around blindly. "What the hell is going on! Did we get them? Is everyone okay?" Rufus accidentally picked off some of his gang with his blind shots.

In the confusion, Ava and Molly managed to grab a couple of discarded bikes.

"Now what?" said Molly.

"Go the way the bus was heading. I'll go the other way, split them up. We'll meet up with you later."

"What, but how?"

But Ava already throttled a chopper and launched away in a cloud of smoke. Molly was about to do the same, she revved up her bike when she felt something grab her from behind.

Slint held a knife to her neck. "Now where do you think you're going, little lady?"

Molly elbowed Slint in the chest, broke his grip, and shouted "I don't know!" Then, she pushed him in front of a speeding stray motorcycle.

The bike ran right over Slint. He didn't try to get up after that, he just moaned.

Molly throttled the chopper and tore ass outta there.

In the cloud of smoke, Slint shouted, "Rufus, they're getting away."

"Well, follow them, dammit!"

Slint struggled to his feet. "Which one, they split up?"

"Well, split up and follow both of them, dammit. Now come on, let's go, let's go, let's go!"

"Yes, sir." Slint turned to the rest of the gang. "You heard Rufus, split up and follow them!"

Molly was a half-mile down the road before she saw the firework chase party start after her. She wasn't sure how long this road ran on for, but somehow, she knew it ended in gates.

She rode down the stretch for hours and hours, and so did the bikers. She wasn't able to gain any distance from them. A half-mile, what was that? Maybe a thirty-second difference? If she let off the gas for even a second, she knew that that gap would close fast.

Thirty seconds. When I get there, I'll have thirty seconds. She only had two bullets left and there were more than two bikers on her tail. Thirty seconds is all I'll get, she thought.
She rode on for hours and hours and hours, and for all those hours she rode, the sun never rose. There were only fireworks.

.

18.

In another life, Glennis had previously traveled down this never-ending stretch of road, seeking the same destination and praying for it to find her before death came knocking. Just like her mother before her, and her mother's mother, all the way down to the tree's snaking roots. Back to the beginning.

In those days, before the concrete layers and de-foresters marred Mother Earth in a foolish bid for control and convenience, the trail cut through Appalachian backcountry. The dense hem of brush and oppressive choke overgrowth posed a significant threat to those who ventured there, but even with a solid road underfoot, the journey was no less perilous, no less difficult.

The Waypoint didn't exist as coordinates on a map. There were no mile-markers or landmarks or any marks perceivable to the human mind for that matter to denote its existence. It was accessed through feeling alone, a temporal place remembered through the veiled haze of memories passed down through generations and gut instinct. But even if you didn't know where to go, even if no one had ever told you the trick to getting there, when the Waypoint came calling, you had no choice but to answer.

Glennis had discovered that the hard way. Years of drowning out the strange, caustic declarations of repentance ping-ponging in her head and ignoring the shadows that twitched at the edge of her vision set her on edge. Fragmented by fear and rage, she resisted. And what for? *Your time will come,* her mother would say. *No sense fighting it.*

Then the hallucinations began—or had they always been? She could never be certain—and the nightmares taunted her, the sweat-drenched paranoia bleeding into waking life, like ink in water. Creatures from her nightmares crawled out from under the bed, mouths dripping gore and talons aching to shred flesh and bone. The sun would always rise just before the first strike, and little Glennis would blink back tears in a cheerful, sun-fed room with nothing but the sound of her own fluttering heart keeping her company. Until one day, it didn't.

She'd fled then, her bare feet slipping over the dew-wet lawn and the cold, early morning air seeping into her bones. She didn't stop when the road ended and gravel bit her flesh, certain the man with scars like fault lines mapped across his face would be at her heels, ready to drag her off to hell. She stumbled into Waypoint numb and exhausted, but safe, relatively speaking.

The land demanded payment, and in the end, it always got its due.

Her second trip to the Waypoint was a mistake and one that she would take with her to the grave.

**

"Do no harm" was bullshit. Glennis adopted it as a mantra early on, letting the words curl around her like the oversized shawls her mother used to knit in winter. Existence was harm to someone or something else, no getting around it. Magic was no different. And if she wanted to use the gifts that flowed like poison in their veins, she had to learn to accept it.

Her daughter, bless her, preferred the shallow solace offered by crystals and oils and whatever useless bric-a-brac she'd dug up from god knows where. She'd tick off the properties on her fingers like recounting a grocery list. *Protection. Healing, Peace.* As though the weeks and sometimes years of sobriety and clean eating were enough to erase the harm she'd already caused.

"Sometimes protection means hurting someone else before they get the chance to hurt you," Glennis would say. "You've got to look out for yourself now that you're with child."

"So cynical, mama," she'd say. "Like you think the whole world is out to get you."

"That's because it is," Glennis would say in response and the silence would gently pull apart the conversation bit by bit until it dissolved altogether, widening the gulf between them. If not for Molly, it likely would have swallowed them both whole.

Darlene might not believe in legacy, but that wouldn't stop the truth. The land would come for her, too. The price would need to be paid. And Glennis knew that sometimes the cost went beyond what you could offer.

**

The blue light ebbed and flowed, pulsing in tandem with the migraine blooming behind Glennis' right eye. How had she gotten here? How long had she been here?

Before her, the landscape stretched infinitely until horizon and land united as a pinprick of light in the distance. Fog lay heavy on the ground, shrouding her footsteps. She didn't need to see; she'd already been here once before. Glennis knew this place as intimately as she knew her childhood home.

As she walked, the ground rose to meet her. The fog rippled out from her swishing skirt, little shockwaves spreading on forever, as far as the eye could see. Finally, a mountain came into view, towering to the heavens. Her steps carried her further, faster. *Hurry*, they seemed to say. *Hungry*, they whispered in the back of her skull.

Step. She leapt across the vast expanse of emptiness and stood at the mountain's base. *Step.* Inside now, at the mountain's hollow core. *Step.* Down, down, deep into the Earth. Heat shimmered in the air around her, but she felt nothing. *Step.* Here, the altar, awaiting sacrifice. But she wasn't here to give. No, she was tired of giving.

Today, she would take what she—what her family—deserved.

Losing her husband had been the final straw. Watching spell after spell fizzle as his brain gradually slipped away had been an offense too great to bear. The Hammersmiths had not bled so much for so long to remain so powerless.

From a scarf tied around her waist, Glennis produced a small, gilded vial. She uncorked the stopper and sprinkled the dull, gray ash over the rust-colored stone altar. She spoke a spell into the shining pendant around her neck. It glowed softly at her words. *Receptive.* The thought tickled her ear, and so she continued to pour her heart into her hands, emotion building with the fall of each hard syllable.

A crack like lightning filled the cavernous chamber. Glennis flung her hands up to shield her eyes from a flash of blue light.

Do not betray us again. The thought echoed in her skull, and she fought down a wave of nausea.

On the altar sat an obsidian sphere. Carefully, she placed her fingers on the glossy surface and was surprised to find it warm. She held her breath and waited. There! The *thu-thump* of a tiny beating heart. She let out an exhausted sigh and crumpled to the ground as the mountain melted away from her.

It worked. So long as the familiar lived, they would be safe. Relatively speaking.

19.

Rufus was a handsome man, once. Or so he preferred to tell himself. And as his motorcycle complained beneath him, the dim speck of a fleeing Molly at the far edge of his vision, he thought of his once-magnificent appearance, the warm companion to the drawly charm he exuded through every conversation. The fact was, Molly was the ticket back to glory. At least, that's what Nash said, with aged gestures to him and the rest of the gang. His gang. But first, you need to scrabble through thick and country and bring back what was lost. The cost of meddling with things you don't quite understand, son, Nash had said. Like he was a child. Rufus flexed the thick, bulbous fingers of his right hand on the throttle and felt a gas pocket of shame settle in his gut.

But damn, he thought, how long was it since those handsome days? Where do the horses end, and the gassed-up wheels begin? Another goddamn life.

One of the boys had used that phrase in the morning as they refueled their birds outside some greasy spoon.

"No luck with that last bus," Slint said.

Rufus said, "Not a damn bit. Used to be, we had all the luck. You 'member that?"

"Another goddamn life."

Rufus peeked over his head. Some of the boys were busying themselves in front of a dusty vending machine. The morning light made it look like some blinded mirror. Rufus felt his lone eye burn behind the single-lens sunglasses he wore.

"Gonna hit the head," he said, partly to Slint, partly to no one. He stepped into the diner and felt eyes on him. Despite having a lone eye Rufus possessed terrific vision—well, except during the pain spells, like that moment, but he could still see alright -- and the half-handful of diner occupants seemed to recoil as though they'd been struck. A waiter near the counter looked as though he was about to climb into the pot of coffee he held to hide. Rufus clicked his teeth at the man and jabbed a finger-gun in his direction before pushing his big frame through the door of the bathroom. The slam of the door against the tiled bathroom wall echoed through the dim dank. Rufus stepped up to the mirror and pulled the single-lens glasses away. His eye had never looked healthy, to begin with; usually jagged by bright-red streaks as if some permanent tempest was etched across them. But at that moment, blotchy purple-black spots threatened to invade the iris, and without the glasses, the pungency emanating from them was clearer. His eye was actively rotting. Rufus took a small pouch from one of his pockets and removed a pinch of salt. Cut with what looked like glass shards colored pink and green. He grimaced and, using his free hand to hold his eye wide open, sprinkled the mixture onto it. Inside him bloomed a halo of pain. He bent, grubby fingers like loose ship lashings on the sink, his movement too swift to stop himself from plowing his knee against the floor. He was far from the pain. As before he wasn't in the present but in a room over a saloon as cacophonous cackles bolted up the stairs. An old woman's hands vultured his, she asking *what is it you want* and Rufus demanding whatever it took to be the fastest, even if he had to thrust hot-nail wings to his feet if it meant he could fly, bandit dreams of bank robbery that two weeks later were dashed when the promise of an eye, a younger eye, a lover's eye because he was too jaded to be useful, could not be repaid. So, she took his eye and more. Now there he was, a few lives later, the pain lingering on his face like week-old terrible news.

He raised himself on his damn-near useless legs, then sauntered back out through the diner. Rufus Stillborn flashed some finger-guns again, but the weapons of his long-aborted charm were weak, and they shook, and when he passed back into the open dusty air, he felt a blanket of relief that the interaction was over. He snarled some consonants and strode toward his chopper. The gang followed suit and for a brief but not quite sympathetic flash, he knew they, too, carried their respective curses in leather satchel bags and pouches lashed to their seats. They were stray dogs who gnashed and lashed out just enough to hide the fact that they answered some phantom master who now demanded a girl, another damn young life thought Rufus. Maybe if he got this girl the whole damn thing would end, and he could die, and the wheel would at last stop its spin. Rufus resurrected his bike with a kick and howled back onto the highway.

It took some hours, but they caught up with the shape after they passed through some nondescript villages and long stretches of farmland highway. As he approached from the spear-tip of the gang he loosened a chain from inside his sleeve, ready to catch a snag and bring this chase to a conclusion. But it wasn't her. Some young couple, guppy-eyed, gripping each other atop their puttering bike, gazed at him through goggles as he stared dumbfounded from his ride. What the hell was this? he thought. Rufus bellowed and tugged his bike to the roadside. He seethed as the rest of the gang formed a bulbous half-U around him.

"What the hell?" Slint asked.

"It wasn't her," Rufus sputtered. He reached into his coat and pulled out the tattered remnants of an old cigar. He stuck it between his lips and soon it sprouted smoke like some broken chimney. Rufus greedily swallowed its offerings.

"It wasn't her, goddamnit!" he shouted.

"How is that possible? We had eyes on her the whole time."

"I don't know. Maybe some kind of spell. An illusion. Or maybe we're all goddamn stupid. Or maybe the other group's got the right lead."

Rufus looked back to the road. The farmland around them glowed beneath the day's looming conclusion. Salvation's promise felt more distant now. The girl was gone. There would be questions, from Nash, from the others. As Rufus spat his cigar into the dirt, he masked a smile with a grubby hand, a tiny part of him glad, almost, that she had found a way to vanish.

20.

Comparatively speaking, held up to what Molly had just witnessed, her mother was not a monster. Drinking too much too often was common, has been. Darleen got mainly quiet from booze, and, when drunk during business hours, was prone to buying small gifts for Molly. It took some maturing on Molly's part not to associate her mother's bad habits with generosity.

And in this space of the head-start, with the monsters on motorcycles out of her line of sight, Molly was back in her codependent relationship with reality. She took brief pleasure in considering herself to be the weirdest thing she knew of. Of course, this idea was shattered, but not yet pushed out of the frame onto the floor in pieces. It was quirky and brave that she took that job at the cemetery, right? She should be admired for not drinking like her mother. Cutting herself gave her some kind of power.

Ridiculous. She had no insight into how the world worked. That man had one eye. She might now join the Women Who Scream.

Molly knew from her travels from Kentucky to Georgia that much of this country was filled with nothing. The interstate project had been successful, but not in filling in the gaps. Her motorcycle continued to work, but it wouldn't forever. This landscape was impossible to romanticize. She had not heard of the desert of the Deep South.

Demons tested saints in the desert. This is their preferred arena, most likely because there seems to be no hope. And that test was usually a temptation, an offer to immediately escape whatever difficult situation the Saint found herself in. Molly was aware of this from bible study Darlene had dropped her off a few times as a form of childcare. But because of her mother's erratic, boozy scheduling, Molly's knowledge of the gospel was skewed.

For instance, she missed the Sermon on the Mount completely but was present to learn about Jesus' grand finale, that holy ghoul.

What would be Nash and his cohort's offer to end this? Would she accept?

And there was her mother in the middle of the haunted desert road.

There's a psychic and somatic space about two or three drinks, and that's where this Darlene appeared to be. She was smiling, leaning a bit, holding a martini glass among the arid boredom, and this was Molly's second or third clue that this was some fiend and not exactly her mother. Darlene, though a fan of gin, never made martinis. She preferred to mix with powdered lemonade.

Molly did not stop.

Once, back in Kentucky, she had driven past her mother being held up by two strange men coming out of the bar. She could not bring herself to stop then either.

Molly believed that something would appear on the horizon eventually, something normal. This was still Georgia. But, no, it was only more versions of Darlene, smiling, gripping that ridiculous glass. Every five miles or so, there was her mother figure, as if Molly were driving on some small globe. Finally, Molly slowed to a stop and screamed.

This Darlene spoke quietly, "I got you something." Then got on the back of the bike.

The last gift Molly received from her mother was a rock tumbler. Of course, Darlene was trying to inspire her daughter to a similar interest in totems, but the machine was loud and surprisingly complicated. It seemed to be a gift out of another decade. The results were slightly brighter but did not compare to the personal stones and crystals her mother cherished, which seemed to be lit from the inside. Darlene did not touch the tumbler—she preferred to leave her stones outside to collect the heat of the moon.

That Molly tried the rock tumbler at all was proof of something though. She wore no jewelry and did not dream about an engagement diamond. She had no desire either to scour riverbanks or parking lots for raw materials. The gift was typical of drunks in that it was pure and misguided, and met with a sad kind of kindness.

21.

Molly remembers Darlene in a series of absences. Every birthday party she missed. Lessons in conjuring and defense magic, replaced with the casual crystal, promising health and healing. The moments she assumes every daughter shares with their mother are replaced by empty bottles and cans she would learn to call "Darlene" instead.

Molly tilts her head back and pinches her nose. She curses herself for clinging to the hope that, maybe, there is a chance Darlene could still be her mom. The fiend pretending to be Darlene is comprised of what is and what might have been. Her hair changes from the long, auburn curls that tease her shoulders, to the dry, overly dyed blonde strands that cling to her lips. Her skin dissolves from cream-colored, cheeks full, to haunted and gaunt. Green eyes fading until they are grey. Rather than staring at Molly, they peek at the spaces beside her. All the weight Darlene held in her cheeks seeps into her throat which swells, mimicking the long swigs from a bottle.

"I want to show you something," she says. The fiend laughs between the fingers covering her mouth, their nails changing from red to chipped and chewed down to the cuticle.

They are where the road ends and darkness forms. Molly witnesses a car drive into the darkness. She thinks about reaching out, alerting the car to what its driver cannot see. However, the fiend touches Molly's arm. The contact is so gentle yet cold. It makes the familiar tickle in Molly's nose return. Darlene would never touch her this way. By the time Molly was a teenager, she shared an unspoken agreement with Darlene that the time for hugs or any familial touch was over.

Yet, the fiend reaches for her so easily. Like all those years before, when Molly was a daughter in name only, didn't exist.

Of course, for the fiend, those years never happened. Molly sniffles the blood creeping down from her nostril back up. The fiend might think she's on the verge of tears for the lost car. That might explain why she winks at Molly. The car reappears from the darkness, as if spat from it, the engine hesitating before speeding along in the opposite direction.

Molly envies the driver's ignorance and wishes she could head into the darkness. Return to the cemetery. To a life where the fiend version of her mother didn't abandon her just like her mother. Who's touch she didn't miss. Who didn't flicker between a version of sober to drunk Darlene while posing for pictures under a highway road sign that reads, "Leaving Georgia."

"Let's get this over with," Molly says, reaching for the darkness.

The fiend slaps her hand away. "Not yet." She smiles, tears forming in her eyes. The fiend scratches her arms and bites her lower lip. "Not yet."

She flashes between sober and drunk Darlene faster than she did before. Then, the fiend seems to combine the two, sober Darlene with sunken cheeks and chipped nails. Drunk Darlene with green eyes and auburn hair, nails chewed to the cuticle. Molly tries to separate the two images of her mother. Tells herself that this creature is a fiend but all she sees is Darlene scratching her arms until the red on her nails isn't nail polish. The skin peels from the fiend slip to the ground, her arms transitioning from flesh to blood and muscle. With every deepening scratch she repeats, *not yet, not yet, not yet.*

Molly doesn't want to feel guilt for the fiend. Is surprised that she could feel anything for the creature in this short amount of time. All the things she never felt towards Darlene. To keep from going to her, Molly wipes the sweat from her brow. When she finds none there, Molly swipes at her cheek, her neck, and under her arms. She knows something is crawling on her, something she can't find.

"Take a picture with me?"

The fiend stands directly in front of Molly, head tilted to the side. Molly has never heard her mother's voice become so small and pitiful. She gasps at the sound, something metallic settling on her tongue.

Blood from her nose.

Molly turns away from the fiend and attempts to block her nose with the back of her hand. However, her nose continues to bleed despite her efforts to stay calm. The desire arrives to pinch her nose and tilt her head back.

"Take a picture with me?"

"I don't have a camera." The answer sounds like a child on the verge of a tantrum, something Molly swore she'd never been in front of Darlene.

The fiend forces Molly's head down. She pulls a big piece of cotton from the darkness and rolls it up into clumps. Once the fiend removes Molly's hand from in front of her nose, she stuffs the cotton clumps into each nostril.

"Breathe Molly. Through your mouth," and she shows Molly how.

The hot air of Georgia fills Molly's lungs as she breathes as instructed. The fiend no longer flickers or bleeds. The strips of skin she once shed are gone, her skin marked with scars. Instead, she settles for a different Darlene, one Molly recognizes from a picture at the bottom of Glennis's "odds and ends" drawer. Darlene when she was Molly's age, was in red and black flannel, jeans shredded at the knees, barefoot, hair in a messy bun on top of her head.

"We don't have time for this," though Molly wishes they did. Although the answers would be lies, she wonders what she might learn from the fiend.

"No, we don't." The fiend scratches her arms again. Her nails drag over each scar, opening them once more. By the time Molly can remove the cotton from her nose, the fiend has started to claw at her neck.

"Don't be afraid of the pain."

What escapes from the fiend's mouth is something between a laugh and a sob. The scars stretch to her legs and face, even though the fiend continues to claw her arms and neck. "I need you to know," she says, "I need you to know that I screamed."

Molly steps away from the fiend. That couldn't be true. Darlene would never be one of the women who screamed. She was somewhere with her crystals, her drinks. Probably with another husband Molly would never meet.

But that doesn't explain the fiends on the highway. All those Darlene's waiting on the side of the road. Her, flirting in bars, pretending to wash cars for tips, or sunbathing in various parking lots. Darlene didn't have enough faith in magic to conjure a fiend of herself, did she?

"We should take a picture."

Molly doesn't know when the fiend disappeared. She finds the creature under the "Leaving Georgia" sign, the skin healed once again. She switches between the two Darlene's like a glitch.

"Where—" but the rest dies in Molly's throat.

"Gone." The fiend stares at Molly, one eye green and the other grey. "Yet, here."

"What did you want to show me?"

"Beyond the darkness," the fiend grabs Molly's hand. "You'll find what you need to defeat the monster." With every word, the fiend's grasp tightens around Molly's hand until she fears the creature's nails might puncture her skin. "But you'll have to pay."

"With what?"

"Just know you are not the first."

The fiend releases her, scaling the length of the highway sign. She mutters words Molly cannot hear, the darkness that once swallowed the highway reaching towards the sign. Molly tries to run away, tries to call out to the fiend but her words cling to her throat. The darkness envelops the sign and starts to overwhelm the fiend. Her hands are the first to go, her body becoming small until she has transformed into a child. Molly assumes this was how her mother was, a front tooth missing, tongue slipping through with every word. A mess of curls fighting for space on her head. Shoelaces braided instead of tied, wearing overalls without a shirt underneath.

"Don't be afraid of the pain."

"I don't understand." Molly runs towards the fiend but stops. There is no longer anything to run to except the green eye gazing at Molly.

"Don't be afraid—" and then that is gone too.

The highway sign fades to grey, the shadow of a man coming into view. He plants flowers in a cemetery. Molly squints and recognizes the sign in the distance. "Scarlet Maple Cemetery." The man is digging soil with cupped hands, filling the holes with various flowers. He lifts his head, perhaps someone is calling him in the distance. He rises, dusts off his knees, and someone else comes into view. The second man is slightly taller, much broader in the shoulders than the first. He hands the shorter man the second of two drinks. Molly hears the chime of their glasses clink, echoes in the air around her.

"Don't be afraid of the pain."

The sign flickers, much like the fiend did when shifting between forms. Once settled, Molly recognizes the second man, suitcase packed, writing at a desk. As the image becomes clear, a candle comes into view, its flame swaying in the breeze of a cracked window. The man surrounds himself with paper balls, the one he was working on joining them on the hardwood floor. He rubs his eyes with his fists, thumbs tucked beneath his fingers.

The same way Glennis does.

"Keep that up and you'll have mitts in your sockets!" Molly smiles at the memory of Glennis repeating the words of her grandfather. However, as the words leave Molly's lips, they pass through another.

The shadow of the smaller man stretches from someplace behind the writer, appearing on the wall before him. He seems to be taken aback, his chair balancing on its hind legs as he pushes away from the desk. Molly wonders what's changed. Why now does the man try to escape this shadow when they seemed so friendly before?

One by one, the crumpled paper balls sink into black holes until the writer's floor is speckled with pits. The men start talking though Molly can't hear what they're saying. The writer gazes into the candle's flame, back hunched, more of his features becoming clear. He has a beard growing in patches, his hair going in every direction possible. Something in his mouth. One moment a pipe, then a toothpick, then what appears to be the stick of a lollipop. Perhaps the fiend struggles with the details of this moment. If that is true, then why show this to Molly? Who are these men? How did one or both give in to the pain?

"Where are you going?"

The voice causes the highway sign to tremble. Molly looks over her shoulder, did anyone else notice? The cars behind her continue on their stretch of road.

"Where are you going?"

The voice grows softer, but Molly hears the urgency within it. The writer stares at what's left of the floor.

"Where—"

A loud crack. Molly drops to her knees and covers her head to protect herself from what may come. When nothing does, she looks to the sign. The writer clings to a single plank floating in the darkness, surrounded by the contents of his once packed suitcase suspended in the space around him.

"Don't be afraid," but it's not the voice of the fiend.

The writer falls. Molly hears him scream. Feels his fear. Feels her throat ache. Her mouth is open, and the screams of the man falling become her own. All around her she hears their voices. Ava, Benchley, Glennis, Hugh, Ryan. All asking her the same thing.

"Where are you going, Hammersmith?"

And Molly finds, not the man clinging to the plank, but her. The shadow is gone, as are the clothes and the light of the candle. All she can hear are someone's labored breaths.

"Help me!" Who else could be here but the fiend? The sound

of labored breaths is replaced by footsteps. Molly feels her body grow cold, her hands becoming numb. The weight of her body pulling her down. She's afraid of what might happen if she falls. If the fiend did all of this to trap her or, worse, she allowed herself to be caught. To trust the creature, despite everything, because she saw Darlene. No, not Darlene, because the fiend was kind to her. Was that it? Was that all it took?

Molly notices the two droplets of blood as they land on the blank she grips. The shoes of a man, dirt-encrusted around them, appear in front of her. Though she cannot see the body, she can make out the silver frames of glasses and the sharp head of an ax.

"Please—"

The figure before her howls and brings down the ax. The plank shatters leaving Molly to reach for its wooden splinters. The blood from her nose rises in droplets, dotting the lenses of the figure who gazes at her from above.

Mr. Nash.

Something rubs Molly's upper lip. She opens her eyes only to be blinded by the sun. Closed, and she's back within the darkness. Not clinging to the plank but suspended. She was afraid. Afraid that she accepted being a part of nothing, being nowhere, so easily. That Mr. Nash seemingly cut her down and she simply fell without a sound. Without protest. Was this the pain the fiend warned her about?

Molly opens her eyes again, the "Leaving Georgia," sign above her. Her head rests on something soft. Someone's hair invades her view and blocks out the sun.

The fiend.

Molly licks her upper lip and tastes the dried blood that rests there. The fiend must have been trying to clean the blood. The thought of this creature attempting to be gentle warms her. However, the fiend transported her to that place and showed her visions of another Hammersmith and Mr. Nash. Molly moves away from the fiend, and the sensation of falling refuses to leave her.

"What...what did you—"

The fiend takes the form of Darlene at Molly's age. Taps each finger to her thumb, the way Darlene might if Molly only got a chance to know this version.

"Your mother is gone. She wanted you to know that she screamed." The fiend glances at Molly, her eyes flickering from green to grey. "They both did."

"Who did? Hammersmith?"

"When Herman screamed, he was forced to relive his deepest regret. But your mother..."

"What about the drinking?" She can't handle the details of what happened to Darlene. Not after living through Herman's experience.

"A way to ease the pain."

Molly realizes that this fiend is another way for Darlene to avoid the pain. A final message to her daughter without mention of love. No promise of resurrection. No snippet of parental guidance. Not even an apology for all the years she was gone. Not a single wish that she had done more. Molly hates that she expected any of this from Darlene or a mere copy of her.

"We should take a picture."

"Why," Molly says to the ground.

The fiend's hands are on hers. "Because you want a moment. Something to hold on to."

Only when the fiend loosens Molly's grip on her shirt does she realize how tightly she's been holding on.

"I don't have a camera."

"We don't need one."

"I don't."

Darlene had plenty of chances to take a picture with Molly but didn't. Why does this fiend want to know? Could it be...no. Darlene is gone, something Molly should be used to. However, being gone with the choice to return is different than just being gone.

"Not like this."

The fiend nods. Molly hears her chant softly, using words Molly doesn't recognize. The fiend's body begins to change again. Her hair grows past her shoulders until it grazes the fiend's heels. Her fingernails grow and curl, braiding themselves along with the fiend's hair, cocooning around her body. When the fiend opens her eyes, Molly can only see the pitch black of the fiend's empty sockets.

A mistake. Molly should've known not to deny the fiend. When the opening of the cocoon closes, Molly wonders if she should approach. Not knowing what this fiend is capable of scares her but knowing that the fiend could force her back into that world within the sign terrifies her.

Then, Molly remembers the fiend's kindness. How she never let her nose bleed for too long like she...cared?

The hard shell of the cocoon cracks. Darlene was doing a lot of things, but she did send this fiend. Molly is surprised at how easily the nails peel away. Each piece reveals something the fiend has shed. The labels from Darlene's favorite drinks. The red nail polish she used to wear. Strands of her hair dyed in various colors. Molly's stomach turns with every clump of hair she uncovers. The smell of cheap beer and hair dye burn her nose and eyes.

The fiend emerges from the opening Molly creates. She is wearing a blue hospital gown, tied in a loose knot at the back of her neck. Her hair is Darlene's natural color, a deep brown interrupted by gold streaks. Molly shakes her head and tugs at one of the golden strands. Remembers how Darlene believed rubbing lemons through her hair would lighten it.

Molly knows this Darlene. She's the Darlene from Glennis's picture, the only one her grandmother keeps out. Darlene, a few minutes after Molly was born.

They pose together in front of the "Leaving Georgia" sign. Molly leans into the fiend, afraid the darkness might pull her back in. She looks up just in time to see the fiend lean over and kiss her forehead.

"Don't be afraid."

A camera shutter goes off. A bright light engulfs them. Molly clings to the fiend, her fingers curling the same way they did to the plank. She whispers, *not yet, not yet, not yet*.

However, when the light fades, the fiend is gone. With that final moment shared between them, Molly steps into the darkness.

22.

And in the darkness, Molly found no place. Instead, greater darkness. She found herself feeling as though falling. With only darkness around her, its reaches sprawled, weaving as water around her fingertips, wrists, forearms, washing as quick river waters would. Her eyes were open at first, but the darkness proved too painful. She tried to scream, but nothing left her lips. On and on she fell to no destination whatsoever, instead, a greedy abyss to deeper gorges without end, in a descent faster and ever faster.

Moments in her freefall produced fleeting sensations and memory fragments. Tumult after tumult, these memories lead her down disparate trenches of despair. She tasted her teeth with her tongue, swallowing hard the cold gusts: here, the pain of Glennis' recent murder; there, late June memories of Kentucky's rolling hills, soy fields, buzzard-blocked roads amid carrion dinner. Molly remembered those preteen summers spent alone with her grandmother beside the leaning cypresses, every moment in-between lost to time.

Could my grandma truly be gone? she thought, still blinded by the darkness. *Will I meet her again? Is all that—everything from back then—never coming back?*

These remembered totems proved beautiful, mystical; and yet, brief, impossible to re-encompass or translate. Too fast, more memories opened into even more distant memories, these perhaps not her own. And in the plummeting, this chain continued. And still, in the darkness, she reached for these lost moments—perhaps to prove her courage, or more simply to learn from them.

She too felt Glennis' motherly pains, to care for and watch her own daughter succumb. Darlene kept secret this same darkness. So long, so long, until she fermented with it. For a moment Molly wondered if she'd ever be granted the privilege of bearing this burden, to hurt for her child. In younger dreams, she'd imagined herself in the uncertain future; if anything, then as a better mother than her own. No resentment came with that wish.

What of Molly's father? She rarely thought of him and now she was overwhelmed with his absence. He died before he ever had a chance to raise her. He could have saved her. Maybe then, neither she nor her mother would have learned to numb themselves. Maybe Molly would have never applied to the cemetery job, and maybe she would be able to mother a child herself someday. To fall in love. To fall out of love. To discover what she was great at, to build a career. To be a twenty-something, getting it wrong until right. All she wanted was to live, and now? She descended.

She realized that all her life was like this place. The darkness rushed on. Nothing could defeat its pull. And how it pulled! The darkness heaved into different directions, as though its currents were conceived by altogether separate forces, different in vision, yet hopefully to one singular end. She wanted to believe surviving all these strange occurrences might allow her to heal. And if not—

But there's no use now. It's too late to forgive them, my mom...my dad...my grandma...myself, she thought. *It's too late for anything! I'm nowhere. I've been falling for so long and it seems like an eternity, from before I was alive. Here I am, Molly Hammersmith, and I don't know if I know myself apart from this darkness. I was born here. I will die here. Maybe I am the darkness.*

Tears collected under her shut eyelids.

Still, despite this sadness, there materialized a strange new idea. She felt its warmth hold her, caress her, a crystalline shield made of the same stuff of the darkness. This power seemed to have been present all along, a fearlessness that cradled her amid tragedy, a ruthless seed of bravery invested from generations ago. This brand of strength was what offered this chance encounter with sadness, to fight and wrestle despite its grandiosity. She supposed, if she should glimpse the shadow, she could dream of transforming it to hope. Inside her awaited this gift. This believed strength harnessed all her life, this bravery, was taught from words spoken to her by lost loved ones.

It's not too late.

Don't be afraid.

One road leads to another.

Molly opened her eyes to the void. There was still nothing else to see, but she looked down at her body. And she saw her blazing self. Her flesh gleamed. Veins mapped roads in her limbs, all the way to her chest—to her heart. She saw the scar on her thigh given to herself from the box cutter, turned white as a typhoon. She saw stovetop burns on her palms. Every mark is proof of having survived. Every mark is a reason to keep going.

She touched her face and, despite everything, knew she was alive. She no longer fell. Instead, she found herself able to glide along, bound by the lurching tides. She hummed, quiet to herself, seemingly at peace aboard the swaying abyss.

Then, she heard a murmuring noise. She turned to the sound where, in the distance, a bright square hovered in the air, remarkable among the otherwise empty landscape. Treading closer, she recognized the square as a window. At its glass, she pressed her face and could not believe her eyes.

In a room, a figure bent over a table, looking somewhat like her father. He was a young man, most likely a few years older than herself. Gazing at the man, she felt it must be her father or someone related to her, recognizing a webbed hand. With an attentive look on his face, he lifted clunky cedarwood paneling and set it atop boards in a dark room. A series of pitchers and vials with different colored solutions were labeled on a shelf.

Molly had a feeling she was watching something important from a long time ago. She pressed her face closer and cried for his attention. "Dad!" she shouted, but he did not respond. "Hey! It's me, Molly."

Still, no reply. How could he not hear her?

Her fingers found the window's metal latch, cool to the touch, pulling it from its lock. *Click.* The window creaked open. Out seeped the odor of petroleum and various spices.

The man she believed was her father did not see her as she shimmied through the opening, fast under the shadows of the room with him. And there he was in front of Molly, lifetimes away and only steps from her now.

"Well, here I am," she continued. "Your daughter, after all this time. And you don't want to say *hello*?"

But he lingered there, focused instead on the wooden slabs. She inspected his face, noting how unusual it felt to be around her father. Because she never knew him, she felt awkward speaking to him—not that it mattered, since it seemed she went unheard anyway. A thought occurred. *Maybe I should tell him everything I ever wanted to say to him but couldn't.*

"I'm sorry you died," she started. "But, you know, I got this far without you. I—I never needed you."

He glanced up.

She continued, "No, no...I don't need saving. Not from you, not from anyone."

The room's overhead light reflected in his eyes so bright, that they seemed to glow.

It was then that Molly knew he was not human.

23.

Standing in this room, Molly knew this wasn't where she would find her answers, and yet she also knew she couldn't leave. There was no way out but through. That had been her approach since she called Mr. Nash about the job, since she arrived at the cemetery, since everything that has happened since. Molly couldn't find a reason to stop now. She searched her mind for one of her brother's magazine affirmations, but she couldn't quite get there. Perhaps attempting an approximation of an affirmation, the voice inside her head nudged her forward, thinking, "But maybe…" When her mother-fiend talked of screaming, "But maybe," had felt like the closest Molly had allowed herself to scream in a long time. A nagging, itching doubt, masked in optimism. Giving and taking in equal measures, like this tortured vision, hallucination, fever dream, father-fiend in front of her. She wasn't sure what this was. She didn't care. She was tired and resenting the secrets, once silent, that were now screaming at her relentlessly.

She walked closer to this man. And closer. This was it. It may not be where she was supposed to end up, but this could be where Molly found out something that would help her stop screaming once and for all. She knew she would also need to stop the inevitable urge to one day fill the silence with more screams.

But as she got closer, he got smaller--at first imperceptibly so, and then undeniably so. She froze. She backed up, slowly. Molly wasn't used to being able to undo her damage or the damage done to her. The darkness played by different rules though. The rules that had kept Molly safe all these years didn't much matter. In fact, at this moment, Molly wasn't sure what would count as safe and what would count as danger.

She stepped back again. Now, almost back to his original size, the man turned to look toward Molly. Molly looked toward him. Neither of them could quite seem to fully take in the other or their presence. They each looked just slightly away, just slightly past.

Molly started to step back again, started to give this man back his full size, and she paused with the toe of her right shoe ever so slightly not touching the ground—so close that an autumn leaf would be pressed to pass between the toe of her shoe and the ground unscathed, but far enough away to not complete the step. The man was still smaller than he should be. Yet she stood still, balanced on her left foot.

Molly bore down with her left foot as if it was the only connection to the ground she needed. It surprised her how steady she could feel here in the darkness, in the presence of this man that was maybe her past and maybe just a whisper of what someone had once told Molly her past could be. He looked toward her with expectation, anticipation, and with inevitability. Molly would put her foot down, and he would be back to his original size and everything that came next would be as he had expected.

It was this look that gave Molly pause. Standing and solid, she was cognizant of all the years she had not screamed, all the years her mother had not screamed, and all the years her grandmother had not screamed. She could feel those generations of screams that Darlene and Glennis had each carried coursing through her.

They'd all spent so much time avoiding the scream. Her mother-fiend told Molly that Darlene had screamed, the pain overwhelmed her, and Darlene finally allowed herself to scream. Molly had heard this as further evidence of Darlene's failure and weakness. Darlene lost herself to a force bigger than herself, what the fuck else was new.

Standing there on her left foot, with her right foot still undecided, Molly had a thought. The secret could be her power. The screams coursing up from the darkness through her body were too powerful to be silent, to be a liability. So, she put her right foot down.

In what she could only think of as a supernatural game of

Twister, she then put her left foot down. Then, right. Then, left. Then, right. Then, left. The man was gone. The room was gone. Molly stood still and silent in the cool darkness. She had taken heed of her mother-fiend's advice. Even with the clarity she had siphoned from the darkness, Molly still couldn't pin down an affirmation, but now, she wasn't afraid.

24.

When Molly found herself back in the cemetery, she wasn't surprised. She didn't think anything could ever surprise her again. When she made it out, if she made it out, wherever she'd end up— she should have her whole life before her, but it seemed like nothing. It would be nothing unless she took action now.

In the dark cemetery, Molly couldn't envision what would come next. She pictured the ebb and flow of a normal life: Falling in love, falling out of love, having a child of her own, and experiencing that never-ending love. It seemed possible and absurd, all at the same time.

She thought about how the cemetery was the birthplace of everything she knew. Maybe not even what she knew, but rather what she was supposed to know, what she was learning. She saw now how it was the beginning. *And the end,* she thought to herself, hoping against hope that she was wrong.

The cemetery was so full. All of the stones, broken, slanted, ruined beyond repair, stood in rows that Molly imagined herself walking down. And suddenly, there she was. Walking, pacing, marching. Fiends on all sides, heading up and down each row, with a purpose unknown to anyone else.

Molly thinks back to meeting Mr. Nash when she discovered him dead. She tried to bury him like she buried everything that caused her pain. But nothing stayed where it was supposed to. What she's learned about her family cuts the deepest, somehow. She always wanted love but thought it was human nature, something everyone looks for. But now she knows that it all originated here, with Clarence Nash and Herman Hammersmith. They were the origin of her family line, which wouldn't have existed if they got what they wanted. It's only fitting that no one since has gotten what their hearts truly desire. Is it a family curse or just the way things must happen?

Molly knows that she didn't bury Mr. Nash, but his body must be somewhere. He promised her ancestor that he'd die without him, that he'd bury himself here and make the cold, unforgiving ground his home. Molly couldn't think of her own family now; she needed to find Mr. Nash. She needed to understand everything he'd loved, everything he'd lost, and what he was stealing to try and ease his pain.

Instead of helping her understand where she stood, everything she'd learned since leaving Kentucky had muddied the waters. All Molly wanted was to rewind, return home, and leave this part of her past buried. But it was already unearthed.

And so, she paced the cemetery, up and down each row, knowing she'd feel it when she found it. The scar on her thigh tingled and her palms itched. She found herself thinking without thinking of the box cutter, a knife, a shard of glass, anything else that would give her blood and lead her to her destination. Molly pinched her arm to clear the thoughts, looking from side to side at the fiends keeping pace with her. They seemed just as determined as she was as if her wants were theirs. She had to hope that they'd find what they needed before too long.

There it was, the Hammersmith headstone she found before; it seemed like days ago, but time meant nothing now and would mean nothing until she moved on. She was trapped in a purgatory of her ancestral grandfather's making. She didn't know how she could make it right now that Mr. Nash was gone—dead and decomposed—and she couldn't read the headstones to find him.

Suddenly she stumbled again upon the headstone she'd found before: HAMMERSMITH. TO A SON, LOST TOO SOON. She thought of all she knew of Herman, how he'd left to make his own family. And he had, hadn't he? Glennis had been here, and Darlene. And Molly was still here, still fighting to make it right. So, this had to be another Hammersmith. But who else had been here? Why did everyone in Molly's family keep coming back to this cemetery? What was pulling them? What were they trying to set right, and why couldn't they?

Molly heard a muffled cry that sounded like her own voice, but she was still standing. A fiend, she found a few rows over. Hugging a headstone and weeping in near-silence. The other fiends stood back as Molly approached. She willed herself to put her hands on the fiend's shoulders, to pull them away from the headstone.

But she didn't have to. She stepped closer and the fiend settled back on its haunches, letting Molly see the headstone.

HAMMERSMITH, it read, like the other. TO A DAUGHTER, A GRANDDAUGHTER. YOUR TIME HAS COME.

Molly stepped back, stumbling as she tried to get away. The fiends caught her like a trust fall. She knew she shouldn't feel at ease in their arms, but she did. It was the first time she allowed herself to relax since the fiend overtook Annabel. That was the start of all of this, wasn't it?

No, Molly thought of the other HAMMERSMITH headstone. Annabel wasn't the start. And Molly wasn't the end. She could fix this. Finish it.

"Let's get this over with," Molly said again. And this time, her mother wasn't there to contradict her.

25.

Or so she thought.

Molly gripped the box cutter closer in her palm, feeling the blade against the lifeline. She knew it wasn't an effective weapon. It had ended up in her hands as dual protection, not a knife, not a gun. It was simply what she could buy at the K-Mart. She knew it was no protection against the fiend either, but she didn't want to give her last line of defense either.

As she and the fiend both fell in front of the tombstone with its ominous message, she felt a frosty whisper in her ear that chilled the rest of her body. An invisible hand gripped her hand. The fiend wasn't aware of the voice, didn't seem to even hear the whisper.

Molly

The word came. Her name. She didn't know who's voice it was. And then, louder, the voice came again. It jarred her,

MOLLY

That time even the fiend heard the whisper and reluctantly let go of Molly just long enough for her to pull away and run away from the taunting tombstone and the fiend. Molly stumbled a bit and the fiend laughed in the way that only fiends do, a sulfuric laugh that sent bits of flames into the grass. Molly's leg was throbbing and reminding her of everything that lay behind her. The death. The fear. Her mother.

And yet, she kept running because there were also things that she could suddenly see ahead. Her daughter someday. A granddaughter. A thigh without savage red lines drawn across it. A box cutter that only opened boxes.

I am my mother's daughter.

She said to the fiend and the tombstones and the family ghosts that she could feel lingering in front of each of their graves. She heard the crunch of earth and felt dirt clods fly at her back. Turning to face the fiend, she saw the earth in front of the HAMMERSMITH *daughter, granddaughter* tombstone. The warning carved in the marble was glowing. The fiend's eyes were too, golden beacons that drew her back.

And then Molly saw what the fiend held in its gnarled hands. It was the caretaker's shovel, carved with an "H" in the shovel basin. The shovel was full of scarlet red dirt, Georgia clay dirt. Devil dirt that came from only one place. Dirt that had to be dug out in chunks with a steady hand and strong wrists.

The fiend handled the dirt with ease. Herman Hammersmith had never had such strength. Molly watched the shovel slash at the ground until a Molly-shaped hole appeared in front of the tombstone.

Lay down here.

The fiend said the words out loud and pointed and pulled Molly toward the impromptu grave. Molly felt sleepy but she also felt a resolve she hadn't had since she was nine years old.

"Let me help you," she offered.

"What will you dig your grave with?" the fiend asked.

"This."

Molly raised the box cutter. The silver blade flashed in the moonlight.

Molly was surprised when her stalling technique worked. The fiend moved aside and gave her space to dig with the box cutter. Molly began slashing at the dirt with the small knife, breaking up the dirt, tossing pieces aside but not making much progress.

"Dig faster," the fiend said to her.

Molly was formulating a plan even as her short blade dug deeper into the widening grave hole. She knew she wanted to leave the cemetery alive. She watched the light slowly growing over the caretaker's house in the distance. The fiend would never tire, she knew this in her heart, but she also knew the morning light would bring new protection for her.

The shovel and the box cutter eventually began starting to

reflect the sunrise. Pink and orange against the red earth. It felt like hope to Molly. It felt like defeat to the fiend. As the rosy light surrounded them, Molly watched the gashes in the dirt heal. Molly heard the whispers of her family and the forgotten dead in the cemetery whisper back into their graves. The hole that she and the fiend were digging together filled back up and the fiend slipped back into it with a final cackle.

"You'll be back," it said as the earth fell on top of it.

Molly laid down in front of the tombstone. She fell asleep with red dirt under her fingers and the box cutter clutched in her hand.

When she woke up again, she looked up at the tombstone. The wording had changed. It simply read:

Molly Hammersmith

Beloved mother, wife, daughter, granddaughter

There was a single red rose on the grass-covered dirt in front of the tombstone. Molly took off her carnelian necklace and laid it on top of the grave marker. She ran her fingers through the grass and picked up her box cutter to leave the cemetery behind. As she pulled the blade back in, she noticed red earth streaked across the blade. She wiped the earth onto her pant leg.

As she pushed open the metal grate at the entrance, she saw the shovel leaning up against the fence with its streaks of red dirt. She turned to look back once more at the cemetery and saw a specter of her mother sitting on top of the newly-inscribed tombstone, dangling her feet into the grass.

A cold whoosh of air shut the gate, hard with a clank. Molly looked at the gate and then looked back at what was left of her mother. The fiend now sat on top of the tombstone holding Molly's necklace. Her mother was gone for real.

Molly turned away from the cemetery and started walking down the road, destination unknown. She felt the sunrise warm on her back as she tossed her box cutter into a ditch. Leaves and dirt swallowed up the box cutter. A line of blood on her thigh came through her pants. She knew she wouldn't be able to walk far.

A black car approached on the dirt road. Molly raised her thumb and waved down the vehicle. It slowed as she walked toward it.

26.

Molly kept her webbed fingers raised as she approached the black Crown Victoria. The driver rolled down the window. His mouth twitched, and then his eyes, and then an impossible smile with too many teeth.

Molly screamed at the sight of him. She writhed on the ground. The fiend was everywhere and nowhere, slithering into her ear, breathing heavily. Was it all in her head? Molly curled herself into a ball in the dirt, trying to protect her vital organs.

A leather-bound diary flew out of the driver's window and landed in the dirt next to Molly. The possessed driver-fiend raised its hand and pointed back towards the cemetery.

"I'm not like the rest of them," Molly yelled out as the black car sped away, leaving her alone to read Clarence Nash's diary in the waning light above the cemetery.

May 10, 1855
Father finally died today. He was pulling the weeds from out under the house and was bitten by a snake. The last thing Father said to me was to stop being a sissy. Told me to cut the snake's head off and bury it a few hundred yards away. I did just like he told me, but he never saw it. He never did see me. He was already foaming at the mouth by then anyway.

I stood over his body with the snake's head in one hand and the body in the other, wriggling. I wanted to show him. I was proud. His hand had swollen up to something fierce, was the color of an eggplant. I watched him writhe on the ground until he died. I buried the snake and called the sheriff. He sat with me on the porch and held me close. He told me not to worry and told me to sit on his lap. His breathing got softer, and he started acting strange. He made a joke about how we didn't have to go anywhere, that we could just stay right there. When I asked him what he meant, he said he was talking about the corpse, being at the cemetery and all. It felt strange, being a big kid sitting there in a grown man's lap. But I was in shock, maybe, looking at my father's blue tongue bulging out of his dirty, swollen face.

May 25, 1855

I am now in charge of the Scarlet Maple Cemetery. I do not have pleasant memories of my time here with my father, which is why I would like to change this place. A cemetery should be a place to celebrate life, not one to wallow in sadness. Of course, in this case, I have to dig up my father and bury it with the snake.

My first order of business is to plant flowers. Father never let me. Some of the townsfolk think I am insulting the dead, planting bluebonnets and daffodils, but this is my cemetery now. I can do what I please. I have, however, been having trouble understanding the bookkeeping. I never did like mathematics. I have always preferred literature. The sheriff keeps coming by on horseback to check on me, but I don't understand why because he hasn't the slightest idea about balancing a budget. He just sits next to me and watches me do the equations. He says he likes me.

June 1, 1855

The town librarian Hermann Hammersmith came by today. He is the youngest librarian in the town's history. He is only two years older than me, but he seems so much wiser and more experienced. I can only hope to see half of the places Hermann has seen.

June 5, 1855

Hermann offered to help me with the bookkeeping. He is a godsend and my new best friend. The sheriff seemed agitated when he passed by and saw me and Hermann on the porch. He didn't stop in front of the house, just kept galloping down the way.

Afterward, Hermann made us lemonade and we drank it on the porch until the sun glowed orange behind the trees. Hermann brought me a book from the library written by a man named Walt Whitman. The book is called the Half-Breed. It's about the western frontier. Hermann says Whitman is America's greatest living writer, but nobody knows it. He says his next work will surely be a masterpiece. Hermann is amazing. He knows so many things.

June 12, 1855
The sheriff told me to watch out for Hermann, said that he's a Yankee and that he reads too much for his own good. The sheriff asked me why, if Hermann is so trustworthy, he's so secretive about where he goes when he travels north. I must admit, I don't have an answer for that.

It's been lonely here, but busy. People are dying every day. It is a strange business, mortality. The flowerbeds need work, and the new Stonewall plot needs clearing. I am thinking that violet bachelor buttons would look quite nice next to the chicory ... Herman asked me what the bachelor buttons were. I like the way he says things. He told me about the differences between magenta and violet, and then we walked down to the creek and had a picnic with blueberries and lemonade.

June 28, 1855
Herman brought me a copy of Mary Shelley's *The Last Man* for my birthday. He said that in the autumn he will have to go away for a while and is not sure if he can still see me. I became cross with him and yelled. Today was not a good day.

July 3, 1855
Hermann apologized with a case of Sarsaparilla. I had never

tasted it. I apologized to him for the things I said, too. The past few weeks have been a dream. I cannot wait to celebrate Independence Day together.

July 5, 1855
Hermann brought me a copy of Walt Whitman's new book, *Leaves of Grass*. It is incredible. Yesterday we walked into town for the fireworks, but we found trouble. A few men at the saloon called us names. Yankees and nancies and other names I need not repeat. The sheriff was with them, but he did not protect us. We were lucky to get away.

Hermann says those men were just drunk and lonely and said that loneliness is the hardest thing to understand. He said nobody understands much of anything these days. We ended up drinking a whole bottle of whiskey together. Afterward, we listened to the fireworks and the gunshots and the men screaming. Hermann thought they might be coming for us, but I told him not to be afraid. And then we kissed. We lay in bed and just stared at each other. He read me passages from *The Last Man* by candlelight. He always underlines his favorite passages, and these might be the most beautiful words I've ever read: *Deeds of heroism also occurred, whose very mention swells the heart and brings tears into the eyes. Such is human nature, that beauty and deformity are often closely linked.*

August 1, 1855
The funeral business has been slow, and I have a fever. The sun is out but it feels like rain. Hermann said he can no longer see me. He says he has to assume his duties of what it means to be a man, says has to make good on finding himself a wife. He says he's afraid. But I said nothing's more terrifying than losing this kind of love. What else is there? I stopped being afraid of other people when Father died. I wonder if it would make things different if the men at the saloon, or *Hermann's* father, were dead?

August 15, 1855

The sheriff called me a fiend today. He said I have to grow up. He said something is wrong with me, said I was sick. I am going to the saloon to take my mind off things. I need to drink.

August 16, 1855

The sheriff was waiting for me at the saloon. He told me that the Scarlet Maple Cemetery was the devil's playground, told me that nobody in town would ever bury anyone there ever again. He said planting flowers in a cemetery is an offense to God. I asked him why he helped me if it was so devilish. He punched me in the mouth and knocked me off the barstool. There were a lot of kicks and I think I screamed. I do not remember what happened next. Afterward, Hermann came by with a slab of venison for my black eyes. We ate it afterward, together. He was sweet to me, even said he was sorry, but for what I am not quite sure. He took care of me and even gave me a tincture that made me feel much better. He is with me now. I have to leave.

August 18, 155

Hermann has left me. He said he could never be with a liar like me. I don't know what he meant—I've never lied to him. He said the sheriff told him everything—but told him what? He told me I'd end up alone and that I would never be a man, like him. I told him he sounded like my father, but then I pleaded and begged. He threatened to hit me "Is that how you like it?" he screamed, and that's when I threw my copy of *Leaves of Grass* at him and told him he is no lover of Whitman because if he was, he could never have done this to me.

September 15, 1855

Too much drinking. Queer. Different. Strange. Fiendish. A Nancy. The men in town prefer the monster to the man. Why is it so much easier to fear than to love? To invent a fiend instead of trying to understand him? Hatred is borne of fear. It stirs up the passions and deflects the disgust away from what's inside. But love requires something much more difficult—this is what Whitman has taught me. Love requires a recognition that everything we fear can be found within.

September 16, 1855

I am running out of whiskey. Hermann was too afraid to understand what it *actually* means to be a man. This morning a group of men was waiting for me outside of my house. They said Hermann told them all about me and that the Scarlet Maple Cemetery is haunted, and that nobody wants anything to do with me anymore. When they left, a black cat showed up on the edge of the forest. I gave it a saucer of milk. It is now with me. My fever has gotten much worse, and I had to go two towns over just to find a doctor who would treat me. As soon as the doctor saw my webbed hands, he called me the devil and told me to stay away. Damn him. Damn Hermann. Damn this fever. The only friend I have left is this stray cat.

September 17, 1855

It is almost dawn. I have not slept in days. They say when you starve your stomach starts to eat itself. Is that also what happens to the mind? The color in the world is fading. Everything's turning grey. Yesterday afternoon, I saw an old woman while I was pruning the bachelor buttons. She was lingering in a clearing on the edge of the forest. She told me I looked sick and invited me to her home inside the woods. She served me a strange tincture of mushrooms and herbs that was the consistency of mud. She said it would make me see things more clearly.

September 17, 155

Time is playing tricks on me. Something is being revealed to me. I do not know quite what, but I can feel the earth breathing beneath my toes and the dirt singing between my fingers. I am naked in the grass, and I can see the trees in the skies above. But these heavens only mimic the roots down below. I am going to return to the old lady for more tincture. She was right. It makes me feel much better. The sheriff is coming by later to check my books and says I could be arrested for tax evasion. What did Hermann tell him?

September 18, 1755

Hermann, my dear Hermann. How foolish of you to have betrayed me, to have told a town of strangers that Your Love was a monster. And you, Mr. Sheriff, Protector of the Law ... which law protects me from your disgusting mouth and hands?

How dare you call *me* dangerous? *You* are the fiends. But so be it. I will become what you want me to become, what you *need* me to be so that you can maintain your cold, white grip on your poor, wretched world. There is magic in these veins. The lady in the forest has freed me, for now, I know that the worms gnaw at my Father's eyes. But no. It is not only the devils like him that have the right to haunt this place. Oh, my dear Hermann. We could have been so happy together. Instead, you have made me Your Monster. So be it. Your women will not be the only ones who will scream, my dear Hermann. I am the monster that you seek. And with this blade, I curse you, Hermann Hammersmith, and this cemetery. I will give you a reason to fear this place.

27.

Molly collapsed, dazed and bruised, into the passenger seat of the black car. She would've hopped into almost any car with any stranger.

But it wasn't a stranger in the driver's seat; not really. Amon shot Molly a nod and tried to smile. His red eyes said he hadn't slept but his grip on the steering wheel said *let's put an end to this*.

Molly let her head sink into the soft headrest. Relaxed her face one muscle at a time. Her jaw was clenched so tight that the molars stuck together.

Amon glanced back in the rearview for a few hard seconds. For what? *Please, no bikers*, Molly thought.

"Back there at the cemetery," Amon said. "The, uh, the house. Did you see...is he..."

"I won't lie, sir. It wasn't pretty."

Molly thought of how Benchley Jr. treated her the day she arrived. Felt revulsion at his condescension. But she saw the pained lines on the father's face. "I'm grateful," she added. "For your son. He was trying to help me. He was a good man."

Amon sighed. "That boy could be a real pain in the ass," he said. "But you're not wrong."

The car bounced over the dirt road, sunrise creeping through the trees. The wound on Molly's thigh throbbed. It didn't fill her emptiness, though. Not anymore. It just ached.

What filled her now was knowledge. A remembering of something that had always been within her. Seeds that never got watered, now blooming inside her like a tangle of purple flowers.

With the remembering came terrible completeness. A wholeness, like she wanted to run but faced a mirror at every turn.

The small chapel looked so different in the morning light. Wooden, weathered white, no other buildings in sight. Behind it, some kind of farmland: a blueberry patch, rows of bushes stretched across rolling hills. In front, a field of knee-high grass with a creek trickling through it, and beyond the field, forest.

Molly trailed Amon up the dirt path. The iron torches still smoldered.

She saw no one inside; just rows of tired pews, a wooden crucifix behind the lectern. Light spilled in through arched windows. The heavy torches lining the walls looked out of place.

Molly followed Amon down the aisle, and, in a moment of stupidity, pictured herself in a lacy white dress. Imagined Amon as her proud father walking her down the aisle to…who?

"Molly," said Amon, leading her behind the chancel to another door. "What you're going to see inside might surprise you. Might scare you."

Only now did she hear noises, like a struggle. She looked at him steadfastly, as if to say, *I can't be surprised anymore.*

But she was. She was scared.

She was scared because Ava, hunched against the wall in that dim storage room, looked more than exhausted. Scared because her grandma wasn't supposed to be there. Because her grandma *was* there, pale and wheezing, the pendant around her neck flickering like a lightbulb in a thunderstorm. Scared because, between the two women, a young boy was tied tight with thick rope to a chair, staring.

Amon squeezed into an old classroom desk in a corner beneath the room's sole window. Molly approached Glennis, her eyes dashing between the scared child and the two women.

She kneeled before her grandma and steadied her trembling lip.

"She's still weak, sweetheart," said Ava. "Give her time."

"I saw her," said Molly. "I saw it…"

"What you saw, dear was not the end. And I think you know that."

Again, Molly felt a surge of remembering. Of purple flowers spreading and choking inside her. She nodded. Wind splashed in through the window across the room.

In a low, slow voice, Molly said, "Please tell me you didn't kidnap this child."

Ava smiled. Glennis, Molly thought, smiled too, though her eyes stayed shut.

"Grandma?" Molly said. "Are you gonna tell me what the *hell* is going on here?" Yelled at, almost. And when she almost yelled it, the boy screamed.

He screamed the horrible shriek of a very old man.

"That's what the ropes are for," Ava said.

Glennis opened her eyes. Molly's skin ran cold in her grandmother's gaze. As much as she wanted to hug her, she knew what she saw back on the highway.

"Molly, my love, we've got work to do," said her grandmother.

The boy whimpered. He couldn't have been older than seven. Dirt on his face, dressed as Tom Sawyer in a white cotton shirt and brown overalls. Ava laid a hand on his shoulder. "It's alright, Clarence," she said. "You're safe with us. It's okay to cry, though. Crying's good sometimes."

"I ain't a nancy," Clarence said between sniffles. "I mean, I ain't a nancy, ma'am."

Clarence. The name stuck into Molly's chest, cold and sharp. Her eyes met the boy's; he clenched his fists.

"I. Ain't. A. *NANCY*."

Light fled the room. The child's shriek rang in Molly's ears. She gasped but couldn't breathe. Ava's and Glennis's pendants glowed. From them, prismatic light bled into the darkness. The floor shook as the light returned. Where the boy had been, a dead old man sat slumped in the bind of the ropes, a cigarette dangling from his lips. Exactly as he'd been when Molly walked into that house at Scarlet Maple Cemetery. Except, now, Mr. Nash smiled. Except, now, Mr. Nash *saw* her from his too-bright eyes.

And just as fast, he was a boy again, crying into his sleeves.

Ava turned to Molly. "It took a few tries to get him stable," Ava said. "Seven years old seemed ideal."

"This is stable?" Molly said.

"Ava here thought we should talk to teenage Clarence," Glennis said. "How'd that turn out, Ava?"

"Oh, you be quiet."

"I'll tell you how, Molly. Teenage Clarence smelled like he had bourbon for blood. Would've grabbed Amon's pistol if he didn't trip and piss himself. Told Ava here she oughta…what was it, Ava? 'Crawl back into the demon whore that birthed her?' Yeah, that's it."

Soft feet pattered outside the window. Baby blue curtains rustled. A little cat jumped from the windowsill, and hopped off the desk over a startled Amon, into Molly's lap. It purred and nuzzled into her chest. Molly stroked its black fur.

"Annabel," she whispered.

Annabel arched her back and hissed at the boy.

"It's alright, Annabel," Molly said, scratching behind her ears. Annabel studied the boy, then looked back to Molly.

With a nod from Molly, Annabel hopped into little Clarence's lap. Once Clarence looked relaxed, petting the kitten's back, Molly got to work. She knew what to do. On either side of the boy, Ava and her grandma watched her and supported her.

"Clarence," Molly began. "Would you mind telling me how old you are?"

After a shy pause, Clarence said, "Six. Going on seven."

"Well, aren't you getting all grown up!"

"Yes, ma'am."

"And Clarence, can you tell me what you like to do for fun? Play any games with your mama and daddy, maybe?"

Clarence looked down at Annabel. "Mama…It's just me and Daddy now. Mama got real sick."

Molly didn't know this.

"I'm so sorry, Clarence," she said. "Well, then. Can you tell me what you like to do with your friends? Or maybe with your daddy?"

Clarence seemed to think about it. He sniffled and pushed back tears, then smiled. "Sure, I got friends," he said. "Like Eliza, she's my *best* friend." Annabel stretched out in his lap, and he giggled.

"Well, isn't that wonderful, Clarence," said Molly. "Would you like to tell me about Eliza?"

"She's, well, Eliza is…" Clarence's pupils quivered. He gripped the chair. Annabel stood on his lap, alert. Ava stood, her pendant shimmering, and Glennis rose with some effort.

Molly stayed cross-legged on the floor.

"It's okay, Clarence," she said. "Nobody is going to hurt you here in this room. Do you know why? Because we *love* you, Clarence."

"Eliza is…"

Another voice vibrated on Molly's eardrums. From the look of it, the others heard it, too.

The voice said: *You wanna know why your mama died, boy? Huh? Do you? Well, maybe…* The voice paused, replaced by the slosh of liquid down a throat. *Maybe she couldn't take it anymore, caring for a good-for-nothing nancy. A nancy whose only friend was a goddamned chicken.*

Clarence screamed again. The scream rumbled in Molly's chest, and it felt foreign. She'd been warned about what happens to women who scream. But it felt *right*, that tumult in her lungs. Glennis and Ava pressed their palms into their ears. Amon wept.

Mr. Nash sat across from Molly, glaring. "You think this is a game, Hammersmith?" he said, blood spewing from his mouth. "You think this is a game? With rules? That you can *win?*"

Annabel leapt to the floor and tucked herself into Molly's legs.

Molly stood to face Mr. Nash, still bound by the rope that held his younger self. Ava moved to intervene, but Glennis put up a hand. Nash lashed against the ropes with muscles too fierce for a dead old man. The cigarette slipped from his lips.

"Clarence," Molly said, her voice steady. "Clarence, you're safe here, sweet boy. You are loved. You are welcome. You are free to be yourself and you are going to be okay."

Nash thrashed against the ropes and growled like thunder. All the glass in the cabinets and closets shattered. Amon, Glennis, and Ava took cover behind a mound of cardboard boxes.

"Clarence, sweety," Molly repeated, "I know you can hear me. You are safe. You are loved. You are welcome. It doesn't have to be this way anymore."

Nash's image glitched. A dead man slumped in a chair. A kid in Sunday best. A teenager with a knife to his throat. A dead man slumped in a chair.

"There's a price," Nash said, lashing against the ropes. "There's always a price."

Molly shook but kept her eyes locked on Nash's. His growls were incoherent now, spit spraying as he fought the restraints. The first strand of rope snapped.

Molly heard the bullet before she noticed Amon behind her, pistol in his grip. Ears ringing. Gold light, not blood, leaked from the hole in Nash's neck. Amon stumbled back.

The second strand snapped, then another, another. As Nash escaped and his cold hands gripped Molly's neck, Annabel screeched and jumped to meet his chest. Nash collapsed on top of the kitten.

It was Glennis who tried to rescue Annabel. But soon as she touched the old man's ankle, he was gone. Annabel pawed at Nash's bloodless heart like a dead mouse.

Through the window, Molly watched Clarence—six, going on seven—skipping into the blueberry patch with Eliza, his pet chicken, at his side.

28.

Over the next few weeks, they cleaned. First, it was the church, the broken glassware in the kitchen, the blown-out windows. They burned the chair and the strands of rope that had briefly held the younger Clarence, the angry, teenage Clarence, the old bastard. He was set free, finally. They all were. At least it seemed so, and Molly didn't want to talk about it anyway. What was the point? It had happened. It was done. Time to start new, and that meant cleaning, cleaning, and burning and hopefully rising from the ashes, not from the dead like Glennis, but the living present. Stop trying to make some vague unknown thing from life and live one.

They also cleaned the caretaker's home at the graveyard. They wiped the floor of blood and guts and brains. Molly threw away the squirrel ashtray and took the faded landscapes from the walls and stacked them outside for another fire. They demolished the reading chair too, placed it in the pile, and lit it with some lighter fluid and a box of matches that must have belonged to old Mr. Nash. When the fire was going well Molly tossed the matches in, and they watched silently. He'd been dealt a bad hand, Mr. Nash, and had turned into a monster. But who, or what, were the Hammersmiths? Hermann had left him, quite easily it seemed, had broken Clarence's heart, had ratted him out to the others in town. He was no saint either. This was another reason not to talk about it. The thing was over and the whole affair would die, finally, with them once and for all now that Nash was gone.

Benchley Jr.'s body parts were bagged and placed into a coffin, and after some consideration, they buried him in the same plot where the fiends had tried to bury Molly. It seemed fitting to her. He might have been an ass, but he gave his life for her, so she gave him a grave and she would tend to it. As long as she was alive it would not fall into a state of disrepair. When they placed his body in the grave and began covering it with dirt, she remembered thinking when she arrived back on that first day how anyone could allow a family member's grave to go so unlooked after, so forgotten. She supposed now that was easy. Most people's lives weren't cursed. They moved forward. They dispersed. Though erratic, hers certainly had been so before she answered that fateful ad for a cemetery caretaker. And now, it would be work, she knew, but she would finally do it. She would watch over Benchley Jr.'s grave. She would watch them all because she was staying.

Glennis didn't try to talk her out of it either. No point really as neither of them had much in Kentucky to go back to. Molly certainly didn't, and though Glennis did have a house, that was it, and when she was feeling strong enough she left with Ava to see to the selling of it, to settle the few affairs of her life and come back to stay with Molly, to tend the graveyard, to live her remaining weeks, months, years, whatever it would be, among friends and family and with a purpose finally beyond surviving. All three of them cried at the bus stop though because it was the end, an end, the end of a journey, of a time. It was the place where new things happen, where all roads are open and undiscovered, and where they turn after a while to destinations unknown. And that was fine with Glennis, with Ava, with Molly, and they cried and waved as the bus drove off. Amon stayed in the car waiting to drive Molly back to the graveyard.

He always whispered the name when he drove past the gates, "Scarlet Maple," and he did this often while Ava and Glennis were away, well, as often as he could, and Molly would serve him lemonade on the porch of the house. Annabel would sit in one of their laps, and they'd watch the sunset and talk of flowers to plant, grass to cut, fences to mend. Molly wanted a new sign for the cemetery, something done in purple and gold. Amon wanted a gravestone for his son, something simple and set in the earth, not the standing variety, something that looked up to the sky, and he considered often what to put on it but couldn't get past what he'd said to Molly when he picked her up that day in front of the cemetery, and so finally that's what it was.

The Boy could be a pain in the Ass.
But He was a good man to the End.

Molly smiled every time she saw it while out weeding, Annabel trailing at her own pace. There was the flower planting, the woodcutting, the dirt-digging of course. The upkeep was constant for a single person, even with Annabel's supportive meows. The fencing needed new paint. The trees needed trimming. True that Amon was around enough but never enough to help. He stopped in for afternoon drinks and chats, sometimes a Sunday night meal, to stare quietly at the grave of his son. Then he was off. He was lost. Molly could see that. No son. No wife. Sister up north. Molly would see him around town sometimes going into or coming out of a pub, sometimes before lunchtime. She didn't say anything to him though. She didn't wave or otherwise try to get his attention. Didn't follow him to see if he was okay and offer to buy him a drink because she understood. She had gained a purpose in all this. A place, too. Even a little money once Glennis sold the house and wired some. Not Amon though. He'd lost in their victory and was counting down the days, waiting for the end to actually be the end.

The new sign was put up a week after Glennis and Ava returned. They'd been in Kentucky for almost four months and had enjoyed themselves. They went to the movies and out for pizza and beers and walks in the park. They cleaned the house and looked at old photographs and reminisced about their friendship. They hugged and cried a lot for the lost years but felt they were making good the opportunity to catch up on some of that. They were approached by two men one evening at a karaoke bar, two men more or less their own age, and there was some bad singing, some awful dancing, some drinks. There were a couple of dates too, a steak dinner, and even some awkward kissing, which they laughed about afterward. They felt like young girls again and wished it could go on, but Molly was on her own, mostly, and with the house sold it was finally time to head back to Georgia, and they were fine with that. They said goodbye to their men over drinks and held hands, "In another life," one of the men said, and in the morning the two women were on a bus headed back south. Ava slept. Glennis looked out the window and felt like she was going home rather than leaving it.

Molly's plan after the new sign went up had been to advertise for new business. To make a go at more than caretaking for the long dead. She thought she might comfort the newly dead and those still living, but then Glennis took ill, and she had to comfort the dying. There would be no hospital though, and certainly no hospice. Glennis was adamant about that. She knew it was her time, past it actually. She took off the pendant that had been her protection. She gave it to Molly and asked her to wear it, not for the previous purpose, not anymore. But as a remembrance of her, of her and Darleen and their men who had died too young. "Please, darling, for me." Molly took it and at the moment put it on and remembered it flickering on that night in the church kitchen. It wasn't flickering now. It was cold instead, heavy and dull and lifeless, and when the time came a few weeks later to bury Glennis, she placed the pendant in the coffin. It had done its work. It was not needed anymore.

A few weeks after Glennis had passed, Molly sat on the porch on Friday night with Annabel in her lap, a glass of water in one hand, petting with the other. Amon was late, almost an hour now. He'd said he might stop by, but Molly supposed he was doing police things. Maybe there'd been an accident somewhere, maybe a burglary. Or maybe he was doing the other things, the "lost" things as she called them, the pub wanderings. She thought to call Ava to see if she knew where he was, but Ava was always tired these days. Better not to bother her. "What do you think, Annabel? Should I wait?"

Annabel purred.

"Yeah, I agree. I don't feel like cooking for one. Think I'll step out for something quick. Maybe take a look around for Amon in town."

Annabel purred even more.

"You are my little rock of a kitty. You know that?" She patted the cat's head and set her down. "I won't be long."

On her way to town, a motorcycle passed going in the opposite direction. She momentarily slowed as it approached. Her back tensed, goosebumps and arm hairs raised themselves. She veered onto the median. She couldn't help it. Motorcycles reminded her of that one-eyed asshole Rufus Whatshisname. She thought for a moment. Stillman? Stillhouse? Then she smiled, "Shithouse. Fuck him."

In town, she decided to get something to eat first and then poke her head into a few places for Amon. She just wanted to look, not confront. She wanted to make sure he was okay. Hell, maybe he was eating too. Maybe he just forgot. She decided on a diner called the Lunch Spot. These days it was dinner too, as late as three in the morning for those needing sustenance after the bars and before home. She sat at the counter and ordered a burger and fries. Elvis was on the jukebox, "Can't Help Falling in Love." Darleen had liked Elvis. Molly did too. She looked around. There was a couple in a booth holding hands across the table, a basket of onion rings and two sodas between them. One of them had probably chosen the music. What would be next? "Love Me Tender"? That wouldn't be so bad though, she supposed. It made her think of Ryan. What was he up to? Could they ever have made it work? She remembered after passing out in the fire station he was there to take care of her, to steady her, "Wake up, Molly." Could that have been her life? Sunday mornings, breakfast in bed with Ryan and a child or two, maybe a dog and a cat at the edge of the bed, "Wake up, Molly. Wake up, mommy." Bark bark, purr purr, everyone happy. The next song was Elvis, "Burning Love," one Molly had so loved as a kid. That whole "hunka, hunka" stuff in the lyrics had cracked her up. Darleen had to explain it was, a "hunk of", and she always wondered back then what a hunk of love looked like. Not to mention a burning one.

The waitress brought her food and a glass of water and a nearly empty bottle of ketchup. The burger was well done, too well done. A hunk of burning meat, well, burned. She didn't mind though, better than underdone, and the ketchup would help. But just as she was about to take a bite a group of motorcycles pulled up out front. There must have been a bunch of them, maybe ten or more, because the noise was too much, too spread out, and they didn't park and kill their engines. They revved instead, two, three, four, five times, each one a little louder, a little longer. Molly dropped her burger and froze. A few ketchup-covered fries scattered, but she didn't see them. She closed her eyes and shivered, afraid if she looked that single eye would be there. Fuck him, yes, but the idea of him frightened her. The notion that he, with that stupid Cyclops eye, would find her after all this time. Would never let her go, never give up. The jukebox switched to Roy Orbison, "Pretty Woman," and the engines revved one last time and sputtered into nothingness.

29.

Two weeks later, the desiccating heart lay on a stone tablet, surrounded by Bluebonnet and Camelia blossoms, atop the mantle in the Scarlet Maple house. Glennis and Molly went about their business cleaning the detritus of multiple centuries of solitary despair. They swept, washed, tossed, burned, and aerated as best they could. It often seemed as if once they'd bleached out a stain it would seep back to the surface, or if they'd cleared out a drawer of old papers, there'd be a stack left behind that they hadn't seen at first; papers to read for pertinence, to then rip up and throw in the constantly burning fire they kept going in the hearth despite the weather.

The women did their work; their caretakers work, their women's work—no spells would do the cleaning, no Samantha type twitching of the nose, just plain old manual labor. Meanwhile, young Clarence played outside with Annabel and Eliza. He weaved among the gravestones like a slalom skier, smooth and unperturbed. The animals followed him wherever he went.

"To look at that boy, you'd never know," said Molly, as she rested her head against the cool glass of the window, taking a short break from dusting the sills for the third time that day.

"And that's the way we aim to keep it," Glennis was polishing a small side table, the scent of lemon wax masking the underlying stench in the air. It would be weeks, possibly months, before they cleaned it out for good. But both women were there for the long haul.

Molly watched Clarence shaking a leaf in front of Eliza's nose, as the chicken tried to peck it. The kitten watched, waiting her turn. "Do you think he's ready for...real friends?"

Glennis stopped her polishing and came to stand by her granddaughter. Together they took in the scene outside. A perfectly normal child playing harmless games with his beloved pet friends. Or was there more there? Some malice? Some glee for the animals' expense? Would it ever be safe to introduce Clarence to 'real' life? To normal time? To watch him grow from this cute, sweet little mop-topped creature into the grown-up person he'd previously been destined to be, but been denied because he'd been born in the wrong place at the wrong time?

"We still need to wait and see," Glennis walked over to the withered heart on the mantle and sniffed it. "I'd say a full moon cycle will tell us all we need to know. We'll get Amon and Ava to weigh in on it when they come for supper."

When they'd left the church two weeks earlier, Glennis had scooped that putrid organ into a plain old Ziploc, while Molly convinced Clarence to come along with them back to the cemetery. Amon and Ava stayed behind, reordering the chapel. They'd be stopping by the cemetery regularly to lend a hand with The Reordering, but the bulk of the job was a Hammersmith one.

"Two more weeks." Sighed Molly.

"Yep. Two more weeks." Glennis walked back to the side table. Before she started waxing again, she said, "Take a break, honey. Go out there and see what's happening with our little Pied Piper."

Molly walked outside where air like Southern mud, thick and wet, came as a welcome relief. At least it was fresh air, unlike the air inside the cottage, which recirculated like a bad case of hives. She made her way to the far end of the cemetery, where there was a wide-open expanse of a fallow field, where Clarence was busy running in circles with his feathered and furry minions. Amon had told her on his previous visit that the field belonged to the cemetery, so to the Hammersmiths, so to her. But it had never been expanded, no more plots purchased after the scandal that drove away Hermann, damaged Clarence but did not destroy him, and brought out the evil of men and whatever else roamed the earth.

Molly had visions for that field. She had plans. A retreat for LGBTQ teens at risk? A home for runaways? The used and abused? Something along those lines, but there were miles to go, and many spells to cast before that dream came to fruition. But at least it was a dream, and not a nightmare filled with fiends.

"Hey, you," she called to Clarence. "What you up to?"

The boy turned, his face like a sunflower beaming, his mischievous smile all innocence and wholesome fun.

"Nothing," he giggled as he tried to hide the twig behind his back, which gave Eliza free reign to stand behind the boy and peck away at the few remaining leaves while Annabel rubbed up against the boy's ankle.

Please stay real, thought Molly, *please stay good*.

"You hungry?" she asked.

"I could eat," he nodded.

"PB and J?"

His eyes got wide. "Yes please, ma'am!"

You'd think she'd offered him a gourmet meal. Taking this 19th-century kid into the wonders of the 21st-century had been one of the surprise pleasures of this whole undertaking for Molly. To watch him devour a bowl of simple pasta with regular old butter and parmesan from a green canister was a joy to behold.

"Hey what did I tell you about that ma'am stuff? You call me Molly, or Moll, if you want. Or better yet, think of some fun name for me like...I dunno."

"Molly Dolly?" Clarence offered as he walked toward her.

"That works," Molly mussed his hair. She cringed only slightly when he threw his arms around her waist this time, squashing the fear that he would squeeze the life out of her with some demon superhuman force. But hopefully, those days were gone.

As they walked back to the house, she could hear voices from inside. It was too early for Amon and Ava to come and for the four of them to continue their work—was it therapy that they did on Clarence? Whatever it was, it seemed to keep the fiends at bay and allowed this lovely boy to blossom into whatever he might become; boy, girl, man, woman, or something glorious in-between.

"Ah, here she is now," Glennis was putting on her sweet old

lady voice for someone who turned from their seat on the couch as Molly and Clarence and the chicken and the kitten bounded inside.

"Hey Moll," said Hugh as he stood awkwardly, pressing his hands against the legs of his jeans, slumping forward slightly in that shy way he had.

"Holy shit, Hugh," she gasped, "How in the hell did you find me?"

Hugh shrugged. "Where there's a will there's a way?"

Molly smiled. Why did Hugh suddenly seem so...attractive? She'd been through many lifetimes in the few months they'd been apart, so maybe it was because she'd finally grown a grown-up hide and a grown-up perspective. Was it that a good man was hard to find, or that a good man was always there but you were too fucked up to notice? Maybe she'd just been hanging around old people, and formerly dead people, for so long that any semi-normal aged male would cause this tingle.

"Who are you, Sir?" asked Clarence.

Hugh giggled. "Sir, eh? A kid with manners. Haven't come across one of those in a while." Hugh bent down to Clarence's level and held out his hand. "I'm Hugh, I'm an old friend of Molly's."

As Clarence reached to shake Hugh's hand, Molly and Glennis locked eyes. This would be telling. A new person. A stranger. Possible danger to the boy-creature's fragile ego.

"Pleased to meet you, Mr. Hugh," Clarence said. And they shook. And nothing happened.

Molly didn't know if she should walk around the couch to hug Hugh, suddenly all awkward and goose-pimpled and ugh...so girly. She was as unused to her new self as she was to, well, everything. But she knew the answer to one thing, so she asked, "Hey Hugh, want a PB and J? Clarence and I were just about to make some."

"Ah, Molly, you know you didn't even need to ask."

Hugh's smile made sense in this crazy place. This Scarlet Maple Whatever It Would Become. His smile fit in right as rain

30.

The sheriff throws up at the sight of blood drowning the inside of the wedding chapel. The groom can't stop smoking cigarettes.

I couldn't stop them, the groom says. *It was like…*

The sheriff wipes his mouth with his sleeve. *I know.*

**

You don't need to know everything about me, Molly said to the groom, back when the groom was just *boyfriend. Secrets keep the relationship interesting.* He could hear when Molly was mumbling or chanting something under her breath and every time he asked, Molly said *I'm just praying.* The groom learned to ignore it, after a while.

**

The groom can't stop smelling sulfur and scorched flesh, no matter how many cigarettes he smokes. The groom wonders why he and the priest and his mother lived. The groom wonders why Molly didn't have any surviving family members on her side in the wedding chapel. *Secrets keep the relationship interesting*, the groom thinks.

**

Annabel howls in the middle of the night. The groom tries to sleep but isn't doing a good job. Every time he closes his eyes, he sees the one-eyed biker. Every time he closes his eyes, he sees the one-eyed biker pull out a shotgun. Annabel stops howling for a moment.

Are you talking to Molly, the groom asks Annabel. The groom gets out of bed and scratches under her chin, and she purrs. *Why didn't you tell me you were in trouble*, the groom asks the blank space in front. Annabel pushes the groom's hand away and curls up in Molly's favorite chair.

**

I've had a weird life, Molly said. *I don't like talking about it. I just want…something normal, for once.*

The groom tried getting Molly to say more. The groom told her about the only time he kissed a boy, something he told no one else, how he liked it but didn't like it as much as kissing girls, a dangerous desire in a small town like this, to want more than what you're supposed to have, want more than what you're not supposed to have. *My family was tortured for that kind of desire,* Molly said. The groom didn't press. Even if he had, Molly would've stonewalled him, would've stopped talking to him.

**

The last time he and Molly drank together was a year ago. She showed off her crystal collection, the necklace her grandmother passed down. *I could live for as long as I want while I'm wearing this,* she slurred. The next morning, Molly kicked the groom out of bed and didn't talk to him for a week. When she finally came around, Molly made him promise that they would never drink like that again. *Knowing too much can kill you,* Molly said.

**

Take this, Molly said, holding the bloody necklace. *This cycle has to end.* Her last words. The one-eyed biker looked at the groom and Molly and then at the groom. *I'm sorry, but the cycle had to end,* the one-eyed biker said before he muzzled himself with his shotgun.

**

The one-eyed biker had the decency to shoot for the chest, not the head, letting Molly have an open-casket funeral. *I'm so sorry for your loss. We loved her. She was a hoot.* The condolences run together after a while. The eulogy was short because Molly kept her life close, swallowed almost.

**

The groom puts on the necklace. The groom takes some sleeping pills and half a bottle of whiskey. *I need a word with you, Molly.* The groom wakes up and sees a boy and a chicken.

She's not here, the boy says. The chicken clucks.

The groom takes a step and freezes in place. The boy puts his hand on the groom's chest and says *wake up.* The groom wakes up, head pounding, stomach gurgling. He throws up and the vomit spells: *don't try that again.*

**

The groom hears a knock at the door and opens it: it's Ava.

I don't need to come in, Ava says. *I just wanted to say I'm so sorry. But Molly did the right thing.*

Why?

You knew why. Your body knew why.

The groom remembered how slow the one-eyed biker drew the shotgun, almost daring to be stopped. The groom's brain said *tackle him,* but his arms and legs said *no.*

Ava says: *everything has a price. You made her happy until she had to pay it.*

**

Annabel keeps the groom awake, howling at a blank space. He comes out of the bedroom and sees a blood-soaked Molly scratching the cat's chin.

You're not real.

Molly stops petting Annabel and stands up straight. She smiles, her teeth sharper than the groom remembers.

I can be real enough if you're willing to pay for it.

About the Authors

Ordered by appearance

BETHANY BRUNO is a born & raised Floridian. An author of fiction, nonfiction, & poetry, she holds a BA in English from Flagler College & an MA from The University of North Florida. Her work has been previously published in numerous publications, such as *The MacGuffin, Ruminate, Lunch Ticket Magazine, Litro Magazine,* & *DASH.* A 2021 Best of the Net nominee, she's working on her first novel.

P.J. GALLO lives in Frederick, MD with his wife & three daughters. His previous work has appeared in *Apalachee Review, Bat City Review, Indy Week* (NC), *Roanoke Review,* & elsewhere. He co-edited the online poetry journal *LEVELER* from 2009 to 2019. He has an MFA from The New School.

SHANNON FROST GREENSTEIN (she/her) resides in Philadelphia with her children & soulmate. She is the author of *These Are a Few of My Least Favorite Things* (Really Serious Literature, 2022) & *Correspondence to Nowhere* (Bone & Ink Press, 2023). She is a former Ph.D. candidate in Continental Philosophy & Pushcart Prize & Best of the Net nominee. Her work has appeared in *McSweeney's Internet Tendency, Pithead Chapel, Bending Genres,* & elsewhere. Find more at shannonfrostgreenstein.com & on Twitter @ShannonFrostGre

ZAC SMITH is the author of *Everything is Totally Fine* (Muumuu House, 2021) & *50 Barn Poems* (2019). His writing has been published by *Hobart, X-Ray, Maudlin House, New World Writing, Wigleaf, Bending Genres,* & other magazines.

JENNIFER COMPANIK is the daughter of South American immigrants & is a fiction editor at *TriQuarterly*. Her writing has appeared in *Border Crossing, The Evansville Review, The London Reader,* & elsewhere. She's the author of the fiction collection, *Check Engine and Other Stories* (Thirty West Publishing, 2021). By reading her work, you're participating in her wildest dream.

JOSH DALE does well with cats & fancy coffee. A native Pennsylvanian, he's an alumnus of Temple University & Saint Joseph's University. His fiction has been published in *Drunk Monkeys, Breadcrumbs Mag, Maudlin House* & a winner of the 2021 *Loud Coffee Press* micro-fiction contest. He's likely folding books right now for Thirty West Publishing House. Find more at joshdale.co

NICK GREGORIO lives, writes, & teaches just outside of Philadelphia. He earned his MFA from Arcadia University & has authored three books of fiction, along with a chapbook, *Rare Encounters with Sea Beasts and Other Divine Phenomena* (Thirty West Publishing, 2021). His work has appeared in *Crack the Spine, Hypertrophic Literary, 805 Literary and Arts Journal,* & others. Find more at nickgregorio.com

DANIEL DIFRANCO lives in Philadelphia & is an Arcadia University MFA alumnus. His novel, *Panic Years*, was published in 2018 by Tailwinds Press. His short stories can be found in *Smokelong Quarterly*, *Monkeybicycle*, *Drunk Monkeys*, & others. Find more at danieldifranco.com & on Twitter @danieldifranco

BECCA YENSER is the author of *Bang the Dream* (Selcouth Station Press, 2021), *The Grief Lottery* (ELJ Editions, 2022), & *A Constellation of Wounds* (Bone & Ink Press, 2022). Their semi-autobiographical novella, *The Ms. Pac Man Chronicles*, won the *Daily Drunk Mag's* 2021 novella chapbook contest. Her prose & poetry have appeared in *Hobart*, *Bending Genres*, *Tiny Molecules*, *Heavy Feather Review*, & more. Yenser was born in Iowa, raised in Oregon, & currently resides in New Mexico.

JERICA TAYLOR is a non-binary neurodivergent queer cook, birder, & chicken herder. She has an MFA from Emerson College. Their work has appeared in *Postscript*, *Schuylkill Valley Journal*, & *Feral Poetry*, & will be included in a forthcoming anthology with Cleis Press. Their prose chapbook, *Donuts in Space*, was published with GASHER Press in 2021. She lives with her wife & young daughter in Western Massachusetts.
Find more on Twitter @jericatruly

ALINA STEFANESCU was born in Romania & lives in Birmingham, AL with her partner & several intense mammals. She's the author of *Ribald* (Bull City Press Inch Series, 2020), *Dor*, winner of the Wandering Aengus Press Prize (2021), & *Every Mask I Tried On*, winner of the Brighthorse Books Prize (2018). She serves as Co-Director of PEN America's Birmingham Chapter. Find more at alinastefanescuwriter.com

ADAM GIANFORCARO is a writer living in Wilmington, DE. His stories, poems, & essays can be found in *Palette Poetry*, *Hobart*, *HAD*, *Okay Donkey*, *Soft Punk*, *No Contact*, *The Cincinnati Review* miCRo series, & elsewhere. He was an Honorable Mention in *The Maine Review*'s 2021 Embody Awards & a winner of *Button Poetry*'s 2018 Short Form Contest.

AUSTIN ROSS has writing that has been or will soon be featured at *Literary Hub*, *Hobart*, *Necessary Fiction*, & elsewhere. He lives near Washington, DC with his family. Find more at austinrossauthor.com

KIRSTEN RENEAU received her MFA from the University of New Orleans. Her work has been recognized with various nominations & prizes, appearing in *The Threepenny Review*, *Hippocampus Magazine*, *Alaska Quarterly Review*, & others.

ALISON LUBAR teaches high school English by day & yoga by night. They are a queer, nonbinary femme of color who brings mindfulness practices & poetry to young people. Their work has been published in *Moonstone Press*, *New York Quarterly*, *Sinister Wisdom* & others, as well as their debut poetry chapbook, *Philosophers Know Nothing About Love* (Thirty West Publishing, 2022). Find more at alisonlubar.com

GLEN BINGER is an author, teacher, & coach from by-the-beach, NJ. He's the founder & host of the *Betterism* podcast & author of *Head Games: The Novel* (2021). Find more at glenbinger.medium.com

JOHN PADULA is a writer from the Midwest. His work has been published in *Misery Tourism* & *Maudlin House*.

AMANDA DUNCIL lives in Shreveport, LA with her fiancé & their many pets. Her fiction has appeared in *The Rumpus*, *The Toast*, & an R.L. Stine tribute anthology, *It Came from Beneath the Ink!* published by ELJ Editions.

MICHAEL MCSWEENEY is a writer & editor based in Brooklyn, NY, where he lives with his partner & cat.

SEAN ENNIS is a Philadelphia native, now living in Water Valley, MS. His fiction has appeared in *Tin House*, *Crazyhorse*, *The Mississippi Review*, *The Good Men Project*, *Bayou*, *The Greensboro Review*, & the Best New American Voices anthology. He's taught for The University of Mississippi, The University of New Orleans, &The Gotham Writers' Workshop. A recipient of a Mississippi Arts Commission literary grant, he is the author of the story collection, *Chase Us* (Little A/New Harvest).

K.B. CARLE lives & writes outside of Philadelphia, PA, & loves collecting old cameras & snacking on mini–Milky Way's when suffering from writer's block. Her stories have appeared in *HAD*, *Good River Review*, & *Hippocampus Magazine*, & have been nominated for Best of the Net, Best Small Fictions, & the Pushcart Prize. Find more at kbcarle.com & on Twitter @kbcarle

JONATHAN KOVEN grew up in Long Island, NY. He holds a BA in Literature & Creative Writing from American University, & he works as a technical writer & freelance editor. He lives in Philadelphia with his best friend & wife Delana, cats Peanut Butter & Keebler. He's published in *Lindenwood Review*, *Night Picnic*, *Iris Literary*, & more. He is the author of the chapbook, *Palm Lines*, & the award-winning novella, *Below Torrential Hill* (Electric Eclectic, 2021)

MEGAN CANNELLA (she/they) is a Midwestern transplant currently living in Nevada. She is the author of *Confrontational Crotch and Other Real Housewives Musings* (2021). Find more on Twitter @megancannella

ALLISON RENNER lives in Memphis, TN, & loves reading, writing, & photography. Her work is published in *the Daily Drunk*, *Six Sentences*, & *Bastards and Whores*, was shortlisted by *Fractured Lit* & is forthcoming from *Rejection Letters*. Her informational book, *Library Volunteers: A Practical Guide for Librarians*, was published by Rowman & Littlefield in 2019.

AMY CIPOLLA BARNES has words at *FlashBack Fiction*, *JMWW Journal*, *Red Fez*, *The Citron Review*, *McSweeney's*, *Popshot Quarterly*, & many others. Her work has been nominated for Best of the Net, Best Small Fictions, the Pushcart Prize, Best Microfiction, & longlisted for *Wigleaf 50*. She's a *Fractured Lit* associate editor, *Gone Lawn* co-editor, *Ruby Lit* editor, & reads for others. She is the author of *Mother Figures* (ELJ Editions, 2021) & *Ambrotypes* (word west, 2022)

SAMUÉL LOPEZ-BARRANTES is a Spanish-American writer & musician based in Paris, France. He's the author of *Slim & The Beast* (2015) & the founder of the band of the same name. He teaches creative writing at the Sorbonne & gives walking tours & virtual seminars on literary & historical Paris.

DANIEL DEROCK is a writer from the Midwestern United States currently living in Europe. His short fiction can be found in *Rejection Letters, Gone Lawn, The Daily Drunk, Sledgehammer Lit,* & others. He's working on a novel & is part of the fiction team at *Fatal Flaw* literary magazine. Find more on Twitter @daniel_derock

DAVE O'LEARY is a writer & musician living in Seattle, WA. He's had two novels published as well as a collection of poetry & prose, *Hear Your Music Playing Night and Day* (Cajun Mutt Press, 2021) & has had work featured in, among others, *Flash Fiction Magazine, Sledgehammer Lit,* & *Reflex Fiction.*

ALICE KALTMAN is the author of the story collection, *Staggerwing,* kid-lit novels, *Wavehouse* & *The Tantalizing Tale of Grace Minnaugh,* & the novel, *Dawg Towne.* Her stories are in journals like *Lost Balloon, The Pinch, Joyland, Hobart, BULL,* & numerous anthologies. Interviews & readings of her work are featured on *Micro Podcasts, Elevator Stories,* & *No Contact.* She splits her time between Brooklyn & Montauk, NY, where she lives with her husband, the sculptor Daniel Wiener, & their dog, Ollie.

J. BRADLEY is a creative dabbler & cat widower. He's the author of *On the Campaign Trail* (Long Day Press, 2020) & other collections. He's been listed on *Wigleaf 50* twice & Best Small Fictions once.

About the Publisher

Thirty West Publishing House

Handmade Chapbooks (and more) since 2015

www.thirtywestph.com / thirtywestph@gmail.com

You should follow us! Consider being a patron?

@thirtywestph

9 7 9 8 9 8 6 1 1 0 5 0 9